# TATTERED LACES

## *a sister's promise*

## by MAGGIE MESSINA
### *a memoir*

*Elite*
PUBLICATIONS

Tattered Laces: A Sister's Promise
by Maggie Messina

Copyright text © 2024 by Maggie Messina
Cover & Interior Design by Krystal Harvey, Tiger Shark, Inc.
All photos courtesy of Maggie Messina

PAPERBACK ISBN: 978-1-958037-23-2
HARDCOVER ISBN: 978-1-958037-24-9
KINDLE VERSION AVAILABLE

Published by
Elite Publications
2120 E Firetower Rd #107-58
Greenville, NC 27858
Tel: 919-618-8705
info@elitepublications.org
www.elitepublications.org

Library of Congress Control No: 2024908202


PRINTED IN THE UNITED STATES OF AMERICA

*"Dirty Coles"*

# Contents

Foreword by Ray Messina                                         v

Introduction                                                    1

    My Promise                              2

Chapter One: Fire!!                                             5

    Breaking Point                          7

    Trusting the Process                    12

    A Journey of Redemption                 15

    Rising Above                            17

Chapter Two: Danny                                             19

    Letter to Danny                         22

    Reflection                              25

    3/1/2019: First Year Without You        27

Chapter Three: Alice                                           30

    Overcoming Tragedy and Finding Strength 36

    A Fragmented Reflection                 40

    A Poem Written by Alice                 43

Chapter Four: Tommy "Dukie"                                    45

    The Story of Tommy                      47

    Shattered Reality                       51

    Seeking Relief                          57

    First Summer Without Tommy              58

    Last Letter from Tommy                  60

    Last Note to Tommy                      61

A Visit from Tommy     61

Chapter Five: The Enemy Within     66

Healing     66

My Reflection     70

Shipwrecked: A Poem for Tommy     71

Chapter Six: Crossing Over     72

Goodbye, Tragic Past     75

Chapter Seven: Gerri "Mother"     77

Mother's Passing     77

The Backstory of Gerri     79

Guilt of a Survivor     83

Chapter Eight: Father     85

Chapter Nine: In Session: Grasping the Truth About Danny     90

The Only Way to Freedom is Through the Pain     92

Trauma Treatment     96

Unraveling the Shadows     99

Chapter 10: The Truth About Mary     104

Chapter 11: I Am Not Broken     108

EDMR Information and Helpful Links     113

Special Thanks: To Those Who Helped Shape Me     129

About the Author     151

# Foreword

Maggie and I both worked in Radiology at Memorial Sloan Kettering Cancer in New York City during the 90's. The AIDS crisis was raging on and many people were shying away from the field of healthcare. What made it so exciting was working in a career that most were afraid of. For a young man just starting out in life, NYC was the ultimate playground. I went everywhere from Alphabet City to Spanish Harlem, East Side to the West Side. Life was one big afterwork party that never ceased. Eventually, I realized I was the last one at the party and life was passing me by.

In contrast, Maggie was in a committed relationship and a very serious athlete. Her accomplishments in martial arts were well known, but looking back, it was only the beginning. Her martial arts career is still thriving today. Maggie and I were both single when I asked her out on a date. One of our first dates took place on Ocean Parkway in Brooklyn. It was a beautiful summer evening in the late '90's and we went for a stroll.

Maggie excitedly said to me, "I have to tell you this story." She recalled as a child in her mother's home hearing a baby cry but not really remembering if there was one. The reader may be asking themselves at this point, "How is this?" Maggie was one of eleven siblings in and out of foster care. There was never any continuity of residence with her mother, coupled with the fact that her mother frequently stayed at roadside motels. Gerry, Maggie's mother, always denied the existence of a baby and told her it was her imagination.

Years later, Maggie's twin brother Danny was inquiring about an apartment to rent in the Peekskill area. An elderly gentleman opened the door, but there was a young woman standing in the background with an unmistakable resemblance to Maggie.

After a brief discussion it was realized the young woman was the baby Maggie had heard in her home. Her name is Annie and Gerry had given her away in an adoption. The baby's voice that Maggie and her siblings were told did not exist was in fact Annie. Danny had found her and immediately recognized her as being one of them! I saw a picture of Maggie with Annie and the familial resemblance is strong. But what a story!

Maggie and I were married on September 11, 1999. I have had the privilege of getting to know her siblings and being accepted by them. Maggie had two long term relationships before me. The first one was nicknamed "pumpkin head" by her family and the second one "horse face." I knew I had to win her family over or they would simply devour me. Her siblings grew to like me. They saw how I loved their sister and treated her the way she deserved. The second thing I did was to treat her family with the utmost respect and to never judge them. I was told on more than one occasion that they like talking to me. I would listen to their stories and never turn away.

Seeing her brothers, sisters and cousins together on the rare occasion was incredible. The exuberance and energy when they were together was electrifying. They would recant the tales of their horrific childhood with humor, playfully attacking one another, on and on for hours at a time until the morning hours.

They never knew when they would be back together as a group. They were all hardened veterans of a shared traumatic childhood. The evening would go from laughter to anger to tears, always with the element of a fight breaking out. Quite a few carried firearms.

For as long as I've known Maggie she has always given freely of herself to others. Her vehicle is marital arts but that is only to get her foot in the door of whomever she is helping. When we were first married, we would go to the most sordid neighborhoods to teach free martial art classes; most of the times in little neighborhood associations next to a housing project. If any youth organization called, she went unquestioningly and unwavering. No matter where, when or at what hour. Maggie's lifetime of volunteerism has culminated in not one but two Presidential Lifetime Achievement Awards!

Maggie has personally stepped in and intervened on behalf of teens going through a rough patch. I've seen Maggie talk with parents and school officials. There is one in particular that comes to mind. This teen was acting out and was removed from their school. School officials wanted to medicate the child.

Maggie knew, as only she could know, what it means to feel but not be understood and thus given no hand up. She spoke with the parents and the following year; the child was readmitted with no future occurrences of misbehavior. This child is now on a full athletic scholarship to college.

Maggie and I did not have any children of our own. We became legal guardians of a young man named Brett. He was 15 years old when we took him in. Brett's dream at the time was to go to Marist. When we took Brett in, he had attended only fifty percent of his high school junior year. We petitioned the court with the approval of his mother and went to work. Brett earned a much-coveted HEOP scholarship and has gone on to be a successful and productive member of society. We love Brett as if he was our own and he loves us back equally.

This book is Maggie's promise to her brother Tom. Out of all the siblings written about in this book I knew Tom the best. I've got tears in my eyes just thinking about him. We would talk for hours about life, his challenges. He once remarked talking with me is like taking to a therapist. Tom, Danny and Alice are all tragic tales. I knew them all for over twenty years. I believe

Nietzsche got it wrong when he said, "What does not kill you only serves to make you stronger." Each human has a breaking point and when they cross that line, the damage can no longer be repaired. That tragedy of their childhood is foreshadowed by their parents' own dysfunctional upbringing.

*Tattered Laces* is a recanting of the tragic lives of her siblings. Any family that has had to deal with the untimely death of a loved one due to drugs or suicide will identify with the stories contained within these pages.

Most importantly, *Tattered Laces* is a story of survival; how Maggie endured each tragedy, what she was feeling and the means she went to for healing. I have witnessed every aspect of this book and encourage anyone that dealt with trauma on this scale to have hope. My wife has done it and so can you!

*-Ray Messina*

# *Introduction*

In loving memory of my beloved siblings, who passed tragically, due to suicide and drug O.D. during the Covid-19 epidemic, Alice, Mary Louise, Daniel, and Thomas "Dukie" Cole. I have poured my heart and soul into the creation of this book. It is a dedication to their lives, cut tragically short, and a testament to the strength and resilience we displayed in the face of a fractured childhood.

Within the pages of this book, I invite you to join me on a journey through the depths of our experiences. Our childhood was marred by the cruel hands of our own parents, who subjected us to abuse, neglect, and mistreatment. It is a story of shattered innocence and the lasting impact it had on our lives.

As we fought to overcome the pain of our past, we found ourselves entangled in a broken system of childcare in New York State. The very institutions that were meant to protect us failed us in unimaginable ways. This book sheds light on the flaws of this system, exposing its shortcomings and urging for much-needed change.

However, *Tattered Laces* is not just a memoir of our suffering, it is a call to action. Through the raw honesty of our experiences, we hope to raise awareness and extend a helping hand to those children who may still be trapped in similar circumstances. Our voices carry the weight of their silent struggles, and it is our duty to be their advocates for change.

Together, let us embark on this journey of resilience, hope, and the pursuit of justice. May our story serve as a guiding light for those who need it most, and may it inspire a transformation in the very systems that failed us.

## My Promise

I will be a voice for those who may not have one, to fight for their rights and ensure that they are not forgotten or left behind. My experiences have given me the strength and courage to stand up and make a difference, to advocate for change in the systems meant to protect children.

Through my business success, I have been able to give back to my community and support organizations that help children in need. But I know that there is still so much more to do. I am committed to using my voice and platform to raise awareness about the issues facing children in the childcare system, and to work towards real solutions that will make a difference.

My journey has not been an easy one, but it has given me a purpose and a passion for making a difference in the world. I am grateful for the challenges I have faced, as they have made me who I am today. I am ready to continue on this journey, to fight for those who cannot fight for themselves, and to create a more advantageous world for all who suffer.

Just as a phoenix rises from the ashes, so too do I emerge from the pain and suffering of my past. *Tattered Laces* is like the phoenix's wings, carrying my story and symbolizing resilience and hope. I ignite a fire within the hearts of readers, urging them to take action and bring about change in the broken system that failed them. Like the phoenix, my journey has been arduous, but it has given me a purpose to rise above the circumstances and make a difference in the lives of others.

The Home We Remember
Mt. Kisco, NY
1974ish – 1983ish

# CHAPTER ONE

## *Fire!!*

Born on March 1, 1967, I entered this world as Margaret Elizabeth Cole. My arrival was accompanied ten minutes prior by my twin brother, Daniel Thomas Cole. The narrative of my life is not easily digested; it is a tale woven with threads of hardship and sorrow. I emerged into a reality of deprivation, poverty, and the haunting specters of addiction and mental afflictions. Many may wonder why I feel compelled to recount my story, why I deem it necessary to share the chapters of my life. The answer lies in the awareness that countless others are ensnared in the same web of suffering and anguish, perhaps more than we dare to acknowledge.

The existence of impoverished America is not a myth; it is a stark reality that often goes unnoticed, intentionally overlooked by those who prefer to turn a blind eye. Yet, the depths of despair and mental anguish that plague the underprivileged white communities are profound and harrowing. It is not uncommon for many to succumb before reaching the tender age of 18. I divulge my experiences to honor the memories of my four siblings, lost tragically and senselessly.

Mary, my sister, departed on April 9, 2009, a victim of the birth defects inflicted by fetal alcohol syndrome. Following, my twin, Danny, met his untimely end through a fatal drug overdose or possible suicide years later. Subsequently, my baby sister Alice followed a similar path, succumbing to the darkness of drug abuse/suicide during COVID-19, seven months later, my baby brother Tommy took his own life; his demise attributed to an undiagnosed brain tumor nestled in the depths of his frontal lobe during the COVID-19 epidemic.

I am now Maggie Cole Messina. My siblings and I were born into a world tainted by madness, a reality we endured from the earliest recollections of our existence. The chronicles of my life unfurl from the ashes of a devastating house fire, a pivotal moment where the shadows of my past began to cast a profound influence on my present. It was then that I realized the urgency to seek solace and guidance, to confront my demons before they ensnared me in their relentless grip.

## Breaking Point

I always had this lingering feeling of being deceived, never knowing when the next blow would come. This feeling hindered my growth, preventing me from achieving my goals and stunting my relationships, and ability to love. What's even more astonishing is that this burden on my growth went unnoticed for so long. It wasn't until my anger reached its peak that I realized a change was necessary, but by then, it had already cost me too much.

The Fire
January 14, 2014

January 14, 2014 started like any other day. I was getting ready for an event in Atlantic City, cleaning and preparing my home for my departure the next morning. Suddenly, there was a knock on my door. I opened it to find someone claiming my house was on fire. I stepped outside, looking around, but saw no signs of fire. I dismissed the person as crazy and went back inside, shutting the door. However, a few minutes later, there was another knock, and once again, someone warned me about the fire. Curiosity got the best of me, so I decided to cross the street and investigate. That's when I saw the flames engulfing the roof. It was a bitterly cold day, and yet, the fire blazed on. I had no idea where it started, but I knew it was real. I rushed back inside, called my husband, and informed him to send someone to retrieve our dog, as our home was now in flames. Naturally, he didn't grasp the severity of the situation. In his mind, our home was a safe haven, and he couldn't fathom the extent of the fire. Unfortunately, it turned out to be a fire that would irrevocably change our lives.

The night felt endless as we sat outside, watching helplessly as our home was devoured by the flames. Firefighters arrived, desperately attempting to extinguish the fire, but it seemed to be relentless. It was the windiest night I could remember, and the moment the water hit the air, it froze, creating a surreal scene with icicles hanging everywhere. Panic spread among the people, and I couldn't help but worry about everyone's pets. I went door to door, knocking on my neighbors' doors, gathering their dogs and comforting them until their family members arrived. One dog, in particular, was in such distress that I feared it would perish in my arms. This night was like a never-ending nightmare.

My brother-in-law, Jimmy, arrived and stood beside me across the street. We both marveled at how long it took for the fire department to get water. Confusion clouded my mind, unable to comprehend the delay. It was later revealed that the hydrant was frozen shut, forcing them to shut down the nearby railroad and utilize its hydrant. Despite their efforts, the fire persisted throughout the night. Eventually, my husband and I made our way to his parents' house in Garden City, spending the night, making necessary calls to figure out how to navigate this overwhelming situation, and at the same time, we were grateful Brett had decided to leave a day early for college and escaped witnessing this nightmare.

They say a house fire is one of the most devastating experiences one can endure, and I can attest to that. You never truly understand the magnitude of the loss until it happens to you. Everything you've worked for, everything that holds meaning to you, is suddenly gone. People came from all over, offering help and advice. However, the restoration company we chose turned out to be a nightmare in itself. They not only stole whatever they could from our belongings but also our identities. They moved our furniture from one storage unit to another, leaving it damaged beyond repair. To make matters worse, my husband went to their office, only to have the owner brandish a gun on his desk as a threat. They offered us a measly $3000 in damages, which was a fraction of what was actually taken. This whole ordeal turned me into an angry person, feeling utterly helpless as my life in Long Island, New York crumbled before my eyes.

I spent the following month in a haze, desperately searching for a way to heal mentally from this traumatic event. It had taken a toll on my health, leaving me sick and exhausted. I knew that if I didn't take action to help myself emotionally, I would remain trapped in this dark place. It was a breaking point, a moment that made me realize I had to find a way to rebuild and reclaim control over my life.

## Trusting the Process

They say to trust the process, but it was incredibly difficult to do so in this situation. We were being treated poorly and taken advantage of by those around us, and it seemed like everyone was benefiting at our expense. Something had to change, so I made a decision. I dedicated myself to training, putting all my efforts into early morning sessions at Jadi Tention's Champions Martial Arts in the Bronx. I pushed myself, religiously going to TCK for intense fight training. I trained relentlessly, giving everything I had on the mat (becoming World Champion, known for my perfection and strength in Korean traditional forms and fighting). Additionally, I sought therapy and drove two hours each way to see Dr. Rob Sanducci, someone I had reconnected with. I was determined to survive this ordeal and not let it destroy everything I had worked so hard to build. I did whatever it took to protect my security.

As time went on, I realized that there were deeper emotions bubbling beneath the surface. I felt betrayed, used, and deeply hurt. These feelings overshadowed my past, which I thought I had dealt with and moved on from. Through my work, I discovered that it was my past that was holding me captive and influencing the way I felt. Although the journey ahead was long and challenging, it would ultimately change my life forever. The next few years were necessary, but they tested me in ways I never imagined. I began to unravel the damage inflicted upon me by others, addressing my abandonment issues and difficulty in feeling loved and cared for, even when someone was there for me. This self-work was incredibly difficult, surpassing any opponent I had faced in the ring. The fight ahead of me would be the toughest battle of all.

Remarkably, I kept most of what was happening in my life to myself, as I always did. I never believed that anyone truly cared, so I continued pushing forward, achieving goal after goal without looking back. I never allowed myself to enjoy the accomplishments I had attained. One morning, while speaking with my coach, Jadi Tention, the topic of the fire came up. He was surprised to learn that I had lost my house to a fire and never mentioned it. I simply shrugged it off, saying that I would get through it. His reaction made me pause and question why I had kept it to myself. I realized that when I stepped onto the mat, none of my other problems followed me. Martial arts became an escape, a place where my world outside ceased to exist. It had become my sanctuary, and that's why I fell in love with it, initially. I had carried this mindset throughout my life, to the point where I kept something as significant as losing my home a secret. It was a realization that forced me to reflect once again.

What was initially a journey due to losing my home, led to more than I could've imagined. I continued to move forward for the next few years, I worked tirelessly with Dr. Sanducci, who informed me that I had deep-rooted trauma from the abuse and neglect I experienced during my childhood and early adulthood. He suggested considering EMDR treatment, which I was hesitant about due to mixed reviews. However, a few years later, desperation drove me to try anything that could help alleviate the overwhelming sense of abandonment that haunted me since childhood. I decided to confront it head-on. Unfortunately, this decision led to another tragedy in my life.

Trusting the journey meant enduring unimaginable hardships, but it also brought forth personal growth and transformation. Despite the challenges, I continued to push forward, determined to overcome the obstacles that life threw my way. The path ahead was uncertain, but I held onto the belief that trusting the process would ultimately lead me to a place of healing and peace.

## A Journey of Redemption: Healing the Wounds and Finding Inner Strength

In the wake of tragedy, my journey mirrored that of a wounded animal, desperately seeking refuge and healing. The weight of guilt and regret served as chains, holding me back from moving forward. Just as a wounded animal must learn to trust again, I had to confront my past mistakes and find the strength to forgive myself.

My life had been marred by a series of unfortunate events, from the loss of my twin brother to the untimely deaths of my baby sister and brother. Each blow took a toll on my spirit, leaving me feeling suffocated by grief and burdened by the weight of my own perceived failures. It seemed as though my story was destined to be one of tragedy and despair. But, just like a wounded animal, I possessed an innate resilience that pushed me to keep going. I refused to let my past define my future. With the support of loved ones and a newfound determination, I set out on a path of self-discovery and healing.

As I began to confront my own demons, I realized that I couldn't change the past, but I could shape my future. I dove deep into the depths of my own emotions, exploring the pain and guilt that had held me captive for so long. It was a journey that required me to confront my own shortcomings and mistakes, but it was also a journey that allowed me to find forgiveness and redemption.

Just as a wounded animal must learn to trust again, I had to learn to trust myself. I had to believe that I was worthy and had the power to create a new narrative for my life. It was a slow and arduous process, but with each step forward, I grew stronger.

In the end, my journey became a testament to the power of resilience and the human spirit. I emerged from the depths of my own grief and guilt, transformed into a beacon of hope and inspiration for others who were grappling with their own pain. Through my own healing, I found the strength to forgive myself and embrace the beauty of life once more.

## Rising Above: A Phoenix's Journey of Resilience and Transformation

Maggie's journey mirrored that of a phoenix rising from the ashes. Just as the mythical bird is reborn after being consumed by fire, Maggie found the strength to rise above her own pain and transform her life.

The weight of grief and guilt threatened to suffocate Maggie, much like the fiery flames that consume the phoenix. But instead of allowing herself to be consumed by her circumstances, Maggie made the conscious choice to embrace her pain and use it as fuel for her transformation.

Just as the phoenix must face the flames head-on, Maggie confronted her own demons. She delved deep into the darkness of her past, exploring the pain and regret that had held her captive for so long. It was a journey that required immense courage and vulnerability, but Maggie knew that it was the only way to break free from the chains that bound her.

As Maggie began to heal, she felt a renewed sense of purpose and determination. Like the phoenix, she emerged from the ashes of her old life, transformed into a stronger and more resilient version of herself. She embraced the scars that marked her journey, seeing them as symbols of her triumph over adversity.

Maggie's story became an inspiration to others who were grappling with their own pain and suffering. She became a guiding light, showing them that it is possible to rise above even the darkest of circumstances. Through her own transformation, Maggie proved that there is strength in vulnerability and beauty in the process of rebuilding.

In the end, Maggie's journey was a testament to the power of resilience and the human spirit. She showed us all that no matter how deeply we may fall, we have the ability to rise again. Like the phoenix, Maggie rose from the ashes, spreading her wings and embracing the endless possibilities that lay before her.

# CHAPTER TWO

# *Danny*

L-R: Maggie and Danny with Grandma Cole (March 1967), Alice, Maggie and Danny (1977-ish), Danny

On a cold day on December 4, 2018, an inexplicable force seemed to anchor me to my bed. Fatigue weighed heavily upon me, and my mind was clouded with desolation. Despite the unusual delay, I eventually roused myself around 12:30 p.m., realizing that my tardy awakening was an anomaly. Nevertheless, I lacked the strength to rise.

After approximately thirty minutes, my phone disrupted the silence, its shrill ring penetrating the air. Normally, I would ignore an unfamiliar number, but this time, it was as if an invisible force compelled me to answer. My hand moved with an eerie magnetism, reaching out to grasp the device. On the other end was my sister, Debbie, her voice carrying an undertone of distress. I instinctively knew that something was dreadfully amiss.

With a heavy heart, she delivered the news that my twin brother, Danny, had succumbed to an overdose. The weight of the revelation crushed me, and my knees buckled under the immense sorrow. I could no longer stand, as if my very soul had unraveled, and my heart plummeted through the depths of my being. Danny, my other half, was gone, and the trajectory of my existence had forever been altered. This is the tale of Danny, a story forever etched in my heart.

Danny and I were viscerally close, just like any other set of twins. When we were younger, we had our own language that only we could understand, which made for some hilarious moments. I always tried to do the right thing, while Danny had a bit of an edge and liked to stir the pot. He would often try to get me in trouble, while I tried to stay out of it. It was all part of our dynamic, and we loved playing off each other.

Unfortunately, our "carefree" days came to an end when we were taken away from our parents for abandoning us and put into foster care. It was Valentine's Day in 1972, and we were placed with Theresa and Harry, along with our oldest brother Tiny. They were good people, but it was only temporary. The Westchester Children's Protective Service felt they weren't equipped to take care of us long-term.

I remember spending hours with Danny on the swing set, singing and making funny faces. Our neighbors loved to listen to us, and we didn't have a care in the world. But that all changed when we were sent to a different home. We bounced around from place to place until we finally landed with the Gasparino family in Yorktown Heights, NY.

The transition was a traumatizing experience, to put it lightly. I will never forget. I never felt safe in the world again and it took me a long time to heal from the emotional scars. It was a lesson that taught me to trust my gut instincts and always to be aware of my surroundings. I hope others can learn from my experience and be cautious of the people they let into their lives.

## Letter to Danny

*March 1, 2009*

*Dear Danny,*

*I hope this letter finds you well. I feel compelled to share with you the struggles that have consumed my life since you left. It is a battle against an invisible force that threatens to consume me entirely. If I don't find a way to break free from its clutches, I fear it will be the end of me.*

*The void left in my heart since your departure is indescribable. It's a constant ache, a gnawing emptiness that refuses to be filled. Sometimes, it seems like nobody truly understands the depth of my pain. I try to explain it, to share it with others, but their voices of dismissal echo in my mind; Gerri's voice, our mother's voice, telling me to get over it, to move on as if it were a trivial matter.*

*I have dedicated my life to saving others, to being their support and strength. But in the midst of it all, I feel an overwhelming sense of loneliness. It crawls through my veins, tearing at my muscles, leaving me feeling weak and vulnerable.*

*If only I could erase the past from my mind, remove the torment that haunts my dreams. I long to truly live again, to be free from this burden that weighs me down. I implore you, Danny, to take it with you, to let me be liberated from the shackles of this pain.*

*It has been over a year since you left, and still, I struggle to come to terms with it. I find myself reaching out, expecting to feel your presence, only to be met with the harsh reality that you are no longer within my grasp. I have tried to convince myself that your passing has not affected me or my world, but deep down, I know the truth.*

*There is a part of me that has become indifferent, numb to the world around me. The void within me grows deeper with each passing day. I try to express my emotions, but the fear of being judged or dismissed holds me back, particularly when it comes to our mother. I know I must rediscover the fighter within me, the person who fought tooth and nail for everything she has built.*

*Yet, there are moments when apathy takes hold. I question the purpose of moving forward, unsure if I should even try. The pain and loneliness become overwhelming, suffocating me in their grip. I have deceived myself with countless lies, pretending that everything is okay while you suffered silently. It is incredibly difficult to forgive myself for such betrayal.*

*Today, the truth is painfully clear. I can see it as if it were happening right now, you enduring unimaginable pain behind closed doors. I can hear your cries, but I lack the courage to intervene, instead choosing to bury myself in more lies, seeking refuge in escapism. It's a messed-up cycle that only perpetuates the anguish we both experienced. Neither of us could protect each other, and that realization tears me apart from the inside.*

*The memories of those who have caused us harm flood my mind. The camper guy, Mr. Red, Allen Ketchel's brother, Tompkins, the Gasparino's - the list goes on and on. I apologize profoundly for the falsehoods I embraced in order to survive and thrive in such a hostile environment. In my desperate search for solace, I stumbled upon a voicemail, longing to hear your voice once more. It was the one where you apologized for not being able to protect me from the Gasparino's when we were just children. I want you to know that I never hated you for what they did, but rather for what you did. That day, when I laid on the ottoman in the living room, being violated and beaten with a belt while the others laughed and mocked, all I could think was that my life would end. I couldn't escape quickly enough, and I witnessed too much. And when you took the belt and joined in, it felt like my soul died inside, losing all hope. I now understand that it was the moment you had a psychotic break from our reality, your own twisted escape.*

*Danny, I write this letter not to place blame or seek revenge, but to release the pain that has consumed me for so long. I hope that by sharing these words, I can find a path to healing, to rediscovering who I am without the weight of our shared past. I yearn for freedom, for a chance to truly live again.*

*Rest in peace, my twin.*

## Reflection

Through immense personal growth, I have come to recognize that I was never in control of the circumstances surrounding Danny's tragic fate. The malevolent individuals who plagued our lives and subjected us to unspeakable abuse bear the responsibility for the atrocities we endured. It is the duty of the adults in our lives to nurture, protect, and guide us, but sadly, Danny never stood a chance. I often marvel at how I managed to survive, let alone reach the place I am in today. It has been a grueling journey, one that demanded unwavering determination and the simple act of putting one foot in front of the other, refusing to succumb to those who sought to keep me down.

Every single day requires grit and resilience, a steadfast refusal to allow others to diminish my spirit. For those out there who are suffering, who have experienced or are currently enduring any form of abuse, it is crucial that we confront our pain and actively work towards healing. Failure to do so often leads to the insidious grip of addiction and perpetuates the cycle of hurt, as we may unknowingly inflict upon others what was once inflicted upon us. There is no justification for causing harm to another as we ourselves were harmed. It is a moral imperative to break this cycle.

In the end, Danny and I took divergent paths. I emerged as a person driven by an unwavering desire to assist others and make a positive impact on the world, even if it is just within the confines of my own community. Regrettably, Danny succumbed to his inner demons, becoming a predator consumed by addiction and crime. Some individuals find it exceedingly challenging to confront their own shortcomings and embark on a journey of self-reflection. Such an undertaking is arduous, the most difficult work one can undertake, but it is an essential step towards attaining wholeness and living a life filled with genuine happiness.

## 3/1/2019: First Year without you: Guilt and Loneliness

*In the ocean embracing the last moment, feeling of the warm sun and the saltwater hitting my skin, as I look deeper, a purplish/pink appears- this flower is in two parts, identical to twins. Perhaps it's you, letting me know you're with me.*

*Please come talk to me, Danny. I need to know that you're okay, that you're still out there somewhere. The pain of your absence is suffocating me, like a tight grip around my throat. I can't bear the weight of this loneliness anymore.*

*I remember the last time I saw you, the sadness in your eyes, the numbing effect of the poison that controlled your every move. It wasn't your fault, Danny. They turned you against me, made you hurt me, made you believe that I deserved to be harmed. The Gasparino's tore us apart, but our bond was still there, even in the midst of the torture chaos they created.*

*I wish I could have protected you more, prevented the pain and suffering you endured. But I was just a child myself, unable to comprehend the extent of the darkness we were forced to navigate. I'm sorry for not being there for you, for rising above as you stayed, for not speaking up when Mom made that terrible decision to sell you to those men. I carry the guilt of my survival, knowing that you took the burden for me.*

*The memories of our shared language, our unspoken connection, haunt me now. I realize how close we were, even when physically separated. I hated you for the choices you made that kept us apart, but deep down, I knew it was a survival instinct, a desperate attempt to catch your next breath and stay alive. And you did what you had to, Danny. I can't fault you for that.*

*But now, I'm consumed by worry for our little sister Alice. I fear that the cycle of pain and abuse will continue to repeat itself; that she will suffer the same fate/death as you.*

*I'm sorry for not being there more, for not being able to shield her from the darkness that surrounds us. The guilt weighs heavily on me, but I know that if I had stayed, none of us would have made it out alive. Danny, I close my eyes and all I can see is your platinum blonde hair, that mischievous smirk that always gave away your presence. I ache for your touch, your voice, your reassurance that everything will be okay. Please, God, take away this pain that engulfs my heart, my soul. I can't bear it any longer.*

# CHAPTER THREE

## *Alice*

L-R: Maggie, Danny and Alice, Mary and Alice, Alice's Facebook post

Alice was born on October 2, 1968, but her life was far from easy. Unfortunately, she was born with fetal alcohol syndrome due to Mother's alcohol abuse during pregnancy.

This led to Alice having a low IQ and struggling with learning. However, despite these challenges, Alice was the most lovable person you could ever meet. She had a special connection with young children and was one of the most caring souls you could encounter. As kids, I always felt like Alice was meant to be a mother. She took care of our little brother and sister with such devotion that it was evident to everyone.

In 1981, I left for Rhinebeck Country School in Rhinebeck, New York, completely unaware of the pain my absence caused Alice. She cried herself to sleep for three months, and I only discovered this much later in life when she finally confided in me. Alice and I were inseparable. We did everything together, from sleeping in the same bed to sharing clothes. We protected and fought with each other like any siblings. However, the hardest part was being apart from her. Each time I returned home for vacation, we saw each other less and less, and it broke my heart.

To make matters worse, when Alice was around 13 years old, our uncle, who was a convicted criminally insane individual, committing murders, robberies, and who knows what else, kidnapped her. I never liked him and was always cautious around him. It was known that our uncle had raped our older sister, as well as other nieces and even his own daughter. This man was truly disturbed and should never have been allowed near any of us. Unfortunately, our mother let him into our lives, and he continued to harm us. Like I said earlier, he kidnapped Alice when she was about 13 or 14 years old, holding her captive for years.

There was a story that my brother, Tommy, told me. He said that he and our father had driven up to the cabin where our Uncle Sonny was keeping Alice. However, when they arrived our father refused to go inside, and they returned home. Tommy was devastated and lost respect for our father that day. How could a father abandon his daughter with such a monster? But the truth was that our father was scared of him due to past events in his life before we were born. This nightmare continued for many years, with our uncle having control over Alice.

There were rumors that our Uncle Sonny was arrested for his first attempt to take Alice. I'm not sure how true that is, but it makes me wonder why anyone would allow him back into our lives after he kidnapped and raped our sister.

Every time I returned home for a visit, which became less frequent as time passed, my mother would always bring along Uncle Sonny, almost like she was trying to pawn me off.

He would make attempts to snatch me and force me into his car, but I always managed to stay one step ahead. Deep down, I knew how dangerous and detestable he was. Sometimes, I can't help but feel guilty for surviving while Alice suffered. I often wonder if things would have turned out differently if he had taken me instead. But in my heart, I know it's nothing more than wishful thinking. He was a monster who wouldn't have stopped at just one or two of us. I firmly believe that his actions played a part in Alice's struggles and the choices she made later in life.

It's hard to put into words just how perilous Sonny truly was. He would prey on vulnerable elderly women under his care, robbing them of their money and even their lives. Shockingly, he managed to escape justice, evading punishment for his heinous crimes. I still can't fathom how he eluded capture and faced minimal consequences. Perhaps the lack of advanced technology and DNA testing in the '60s and '70s contributed to his freedom. If he had committed even a fraction of his crimes in today's world, he would have undoubtedly been apprehended and faced severe punishment. It's unfortunate that we had to endure those times, and it breaks my heart that some of my siblings met untimely ends because of it.

Eventually, Alice physically broke free from Sonny's grasp, but I don't think she ever truly escaped him mentally. The deep-rooted trauma and abuse he inflicted on her left lasting scars. Nevertheless, she managed to break away, get married, and have two daughters. Initially, life seemed to work out well for my sister. She embraced motherhood and excelled at it, taking immaculate care of her children. However, as time went on, something within Alice snapped. She suffered a back injury and began relying on oxycodone, or "oxy" as they called it, a drug that was excessively prescribed in upstate New York at that time. It seemed like doctors were handing out those pills like candy, and many people fell into addiction, including my brother Danny. It wasn't just a fabrication; the news was filled with stories about it. Tragically, Alice became ensnared in its grip, and the pills changed her. She developed a severe addiction and engaged in behavior she would never have considered if not under the influence. When the pills became unavailable, she turned to even heavier substances, eventually falling into the clutches of heroin. I never imagined in my wildest dreams that my sister, Alice, would become a drug addict, let alone a heroin user. It was inconceivable to me. My brother, Danny, perhaps, but not Alice. And to top it off, she became an absent mother, which shattered my heart. I struggled to accept the reality, even denying it at times, because Alice possessed such a loving soul. Even with the heroin and everything, I still saw that big heart, and it made it incredibly difficult to digest and come to terms with. However, as Alice's life neared its tragic end, she made choices that were expected of anyone caught in the destructive grip of addiction. She did things that no mother should ever do and distanced herself from her children. It was at that moment that I knew she was no longer the little sister I once knew. She had transformed into someone else entirely. Sadly, we had to create distance between us for my own protection and the preservation of my own life. I blame the oxycodone epidemic that plagued the world for this downfall. When that drug emerged, the decisions made by the pharmaceutical company played a significant role. But coming back to Alice, she became unreasonable, volatile, and unapproachable. Eventually, her path led to her demise, succumbing to an overdose.

Alice's journey was like being trapped underwater: The weight of grief and unbearable pain feels suffocating, making it difficult to breathe or find any relief. The protagonist must find a way to swim to the surface and find strength to keep going.

## Overcoming Tragedy and Finding Strength

Once again, tragedy struck. Still reeling from the loss of my twin brother, Danny, I received the devastating news that my baby sister, Alice, had overdosed and passed away. The weight of grief felt unbearable, as I struggled to comprehend how this could happen once more.

As I tried to process the news, my brother-in-law's callous response only added to my anguish and wonder. His lack of empathy left me questioning his involvement in Alice's demise. The thought gnawed at me, but I knew I had to focus on the immediate task at hand - informing my family.

Overwhelmed and unable to bear the burden alone, I reached out to my sister Joan for support. I confided in Joan, expressing my inability to break the news to everyone. Recognizing the pain, Joan stepped up, offering her assistance in delivering the heartbreaking news to our siblings.

With the world grappling with the COVID-19 pandemic, logistical challenges arose. Transporting Alice's body from Tennessee to New York seemed like an insurmountable hurdle. However, I refused to let despair consume me. I took a deep breath, determined to navigate the complexities, and ensure we receive a proper farewell.

Summoning the strength within, I made the difficult call to Mother. Despite our troubled relationship, I empathized with her pain as a mother facing yet another loss. The weight of grief hung heavy in the air as I shared the news, and silence enveloped the line.

In the midst of our sorrow, I realized the love for Alice surpassed any past disagreements or mistakes she had made. I remembered her as a flawed human being, one that was brought into a world of hell. Alice was my baby sister, whom I loved deeply. Despite the pain, I knew I had to find a way to honor her memory bring her home and lay her to rest.

As the story of Alice's life and tragic end unfolded, it became a testament to the protagonist's resilience. Amidst the grief, we had to find a way to get over the hurdles presented by the pandemic, ensuring Alice's body was transported back home to where she wished to be laid to rest.

Upon receiving the distressing news, we were confronted with a disheartening choice: we would have had to leave her in an ice truck in a non-disclosed location, which risked losing her or having an issue finding her body in a timely fashion. New York was a mess due to so many bodies. The thought of her being stored amidst countless others in freezer trucks unsettled us deeply. We were afraid of not getting her back. It just made sense to cremate her in Tennessee to ensure the best outcome. Reflecting upon this now seems unfathomable, but such was the grim reality imposed by the relentless grip of the COVID-19 pandemic.

We had resolved that cremation in Tennessee followed by shipping of the ashes to me was the best option. A week later, I heard a knock at my door. When I opened it, I was met by a man with a delivery - my sister, now reduced to a small box of ashes. It took three months until we could finally have a proper funeral for her, but due to the pandemic, only a few people attended. I was the only sibling present, along with my husband, father-in-law and Alice's youngest daughter, Allie. Nancy, the minister, officiated the burial. As I watched Alice's daughter lay her to rest, the emotions began to overwhelm me. How had we reached this point? So much heartache in one family.

COVID-19 had complicated things, making it difficult to access support or therapy, but I was fortunate enough to have a trauma therapist, Noelle Damon, who went above and beyond to help me. I did my best to support my sister's daughter Allie, and eventually, she moved to stay with her father in Tennessee. I realized that we can't save those who don't want saving, and in trying, we can lose ourselves. This loss would bring the rest of us closer together. Its suddenness highlighted the brevity of life.

My biggest worry was my youngest brother, Tommy. He was struggling to cope and even spoke of not wanting to continue living. It was hard with this virus in the air; we all needed human contact, but the fear was palpable. I spent countless hours talking to Tommy, but I could feel him slipping away. I had to focus on getting myself back on solid ground.

# A Fragmented Reflection: Healing the Wounds of Loss and Regret

My world shattered when I experienced the consecutive deaths of my twin brother Danny and now my baby sister Alice. Consumed by grief and burdened by guilt, I found myself unable to find solace in sleep, sobriety, or stillness. Each day was a desperate search for relief from the suffocating weight of remorse that made it difficult for me to breathe, walk, and function.

Haunted by the nagging feeling that I could have done more for my little sister, I yearned for the chance to rewrite the past. Determined to confront the unresolved pain that had plagued our lives since the beginning, I ventured back to the place where it all started. However, my hopes were shattered when I discovered that the once-familiar house had been demolished and rebuilt, erasing tangible traces of our shared history.

Driven by a deep-rooted need for closure, I frantically searched for a way to confront the source of Alice's suffering. My younger sister Gerri and I desperately sought out the person responsible for our sister's descent into a life of drugs, prostitution, and crime. As the pieces slowly fell into place, we realized the horrifying extent of the damage inflicted upon Alice. My sister had suffered at the hands of a cruel man who had violently beaten her, using his cowboy boots as weapons, ultimately leading to the loss of their child. This person was my mother's brother, Uncle Sonny.

Overwhelmed with regret, I blamed myself for not fully understanding the magnitude of Alice's pain. I acknowledged my own failure to listen attentively to my sister's descriptive accounts of the abuse she endured. In my denial, we had chosen not to believe the depths of the harm inflicted upon Alice, resulting in a profound loss of trust and understanding.

Every day, I awakened from sleepless nights, beseeching my heart to find solace and peace amidst the relentless ache. My heart yearned for respite, but the weight of guilt prevented me from finding comfort in sleep, nourishment, or performing at my fullest potential.

Haunted by the knowledge that I had left Alice behind in an attempt to save myself, heartache intensified. I realized the extent of my selfishness and the impact it had on my sister's life. The weight of her actions threatened to consume her entirely.

In the depths of my despair, I resolved to make amends. I dedicated myself to a journey of self-forgiveness and redemption, seeking a path towards healing and peace. Each day became a step closer to finding a restful place for my aching heart.

Guided by remorse, love, and an unyielding determination, I embarked on a quest for personal growth and forgiveness. Through my own pain, I discovered the strength to support others who were wrestling with their own demons. In extending compassion and hope to those in need, I found a means of honoring Alice's memory and transforming her own life.

The journey was not without obstacles, and healing proved to be a long and arduous process. However, through resilience and unwavering commitment, I discovered that redemption was possible. Bit by bit, I began to unravel the darkness that had consumed all of my family, finding pockets of peace and light within her shattered existence.

In the end, my story became a testament to the power of forgiveness, self-reflection, and the indomitable human spirit. Through this journey, I not only found solace for my own heart but also became a beacon of hope for others who were grappling with their own pain. And in this newfound purpose, I began to reclaim my own life, embracing the healing and growth that awaited me on the other side of regret and loss.

## A Poem Written by Alice:
*Lost Children, Lost Childhood (2004)*

*I remember you from long ago when I was living in Hell built especially for children. The walls of your home were my only salvation. I'm sure you were never aware of this because I never really knew you. This is why I've always known you. But you never knew me. I was a lonely, horrified child with nowhere to go and no one to turn to.*

*Many years later, you don't want to remember knowing me, but I know you. I needed to be where you stood—a place so unlike my own.*

**LOST CHILDREN, LOST CHILDHOOD**... 20?

I REMEMBER YOU FROM LONG AGO, WHEN I WAS LIVING IN HELL BUILT ESPECIALLY FOR CHILDREN. THE WALLS OF YOUR HOME WERE MY ONLY SALVATION. I'M SURE YOU WERE NEVER AWARE OF THIS, BECAUSE I NEVER REALLY KNEW YOU. THIS IS WHY I'VE ALWAYS KNOWN YOU. BUT YOU NEVER KNEW ME. I WAS A LONELY, HORRIFIED CHILD WITH NO WHERE TO GO AND NO ONE TO TURN TOO.

MANY YEARS LATER. YOU DON'T WANT TO REMEMBER KNOWING ME, BUT I KNOW YOU. I NEEDED TO BE WHERE YOU STOOD — A PLACE SO UNLIKE MY OWN.

A Poem Written by Alice
*Lost Children, Lost Childhood*
2004

44

# CHAPTER FOUR

# Tommy "Dukie"

L-R: Maggie, Dan, Alice and Tommy Home for a visit from foster care (Mt. Kisco, NY, 1975-ish), Tom and Sha (1986), Tommy during the time he was a ring boy with the WWF.

My reflection on Tommy's death:

The pain and confusion of losing my baby brother to suicide was like being trapped in a never-ending maze. Each twist and turn left me questioning my own existence, wondering if I too should join him in the darkness. It's as if I'm holding a book, filled with chapters of heartache and despair, unable to put it down or escape its grip. The weight of his absence cripples me, bringing me to my knees in a desperate plea for a sign, something to hold onto in this sea of grief. But there is no closure, no goodbye, just a deep sense of twisted exhaustion. I long to understand the depth of his suffering, wishing I could have been there to save him from the torment that consumed him.

As I stand before the car that carried his lifeless body, the reality of his absence hits me like a strong gust of wind, leaving me breathless and disbelieving. In his home, surrounded by his belongings, I am overcome by the overwhelming presence of his spirit, and the room where he took his own life becomes a sacred space of both sorrow and longing. I cling to his shirt and the cord that took his life, desperate to bring him back, but the harsh truth remains: he is gone, and I am left floating through a haze of grief and confusion.

It's unfathomable to comprehend how a man who loved his family so deeply could choose to end his own life. Despite my concerns for his mental health, the importance he placed on his guns and job overshadowed his need for help. I watched helplessly as he transformed from a vibrant soul to a shell of a man, drowning in sadness and uncertainty. The news of his suicide shattered my world, leaving me on my knees, gasping for air and searching for meaning.

## The Story of Tommy

Tommy entered the world on October 12, 1970, but his arrival was not without complications. He was born with fetal alcohol syndrome, which left a noticeable dent on the left side of his chest. Our curiosity about his condition was often met with our mother's angry outbursts, blaming our father for intentionally causing harm to her during pregnancy. However, we later realized that these accusations were just one of her many attempts to lash out at our dad. Despite his physical differences, Tommy had the most striking blue eyes and milky white skin. He was undeniably the cutest baby, but he was also quite mischievous. Tommy always had a strong-willed personality and did things his own way. He carried around a blanket that had a distinct smell but provided him comfort and security. Looking back, I can't help but laugh at the memories of those moments.

In 1972, as mentioned earlier, our lives took a drastic turn when we were taken away from our parents for abandonment and neglect and placed in foster care. It was a heartbreaking experience, and Tommy and my younger sister, Alice, suffered greatly during this time. Tommy endured a severe head injury while trying to protect Alice from her abusive foster father. He was thrown across the room, hitting his head on a radiator. Tommy required stitches and was hospitalized for his injuries. I vividly remember the day we went to visit them and discovered Tommy was in the hospital. Only years later did we learn the truth of what had transpired during that visit. Tommy, being older and able to articulate his experiences, finally shared the reality of our tumultuous upbringing. Despite the challenges, Tommy's endearing qualities always shone through. He may have caused trouble like any little brother, but he was unique, and I couldn't help but love him.

As we grew older, life continued to be far from easy for all of us. Our mother was in and out of our lives, never knowing if she would be present or if we would find an empty, abandoned home. Unfortunately, this was the reality we faced. Tommy experienced another upheaval when he was around 12 or 13 years old. He returned home to find our mother gone, leaving him with nowhere to live.

Given our young ages, we struggled to keep our heads above water, relying on each other for support. Tommy ended up homeless and eventually found work with WWE (formerly WWF), a wrestling entertainment company owned by Vince McMahon and his family. Tommy's love for wrestling had always been evident, as he would watch it on TV and reenact matches with our brother, Tiny. When Tommy was approached by a man named Mel Phillips, who was with the WWF, and offered him a position as a ring boy, it was like a dream come true. He eagerly joined the wrestling world, which provided some semblance of stability in his tumultuous life.

Our father would occasionally find an apartment, providing a temporary sense of security, although it mainly served as a place for Mother to drink and stay put for a little bit. Mel would come to our apartment, pick up Tommy, and give our mother some money and alcohol. She willingly allowed this arrangement, as it was not an unfamiliar situation for her.

Unfortunately, this exploitation and neglect had dire consequences for Tommy. He remained with the WWF for several years, during which it became public knowledge that there was sexual abuse occurring within the organization, amongst other things. Tommy was one of the victims, and despite his courage in speaking out, he was vilified and labeled a liar. This pivotal moment in his life left a lasting impact, constantly resurfacing whenever he tried to distance himself from the scandal. Reporters would hound him for interviews, further exacerbating his pain.

Despite the challenges, Tommy managed to find love and get married. He longed for a peaceful life, free from the constant reminders of his past and the WWF scandal. Unfortunately, our brother, Tiny, could not let go of the past and continually sought financial gain from the situation.

Tommy's desire to shield his children from the stigma attached to his name became increasingly difficult in the digital age. Online searches would inevitably lead to the exposure of his painful history, causing him immense distress. As his teenage daughters grew older and prepared for college, it stirred up unresolved emotions for all of us. It weighed heavily on Tommy, who had been a devoted father, providing his girls with a life he never experienced himself. He showered them with love and attention, creating cherished memories and offering them everything he could.

Witnessing the attempts to tarnish Tommy's reputation and distort his true character deeply troubled me. I felt compelled to protect his legacy and be there for his daughters, almost as if I needed to fill his shoes. For a significant period of time following his death, I dedicated myself to this role. However, I eventually realized that I was losing myself in the process. It became clear that if I did not prioritize my own well-being, I would not be able to continue supporting his girls effectively.

## Shattered Reality

The weight of grief settled upon me like a suffocating fog as I drove to my brother Tommy's house. The news of his suicide had torn through my soul, leaving me reeling in disbelief. How could someone who loved his family so deeply, who was devoted to their well-being, choose to end his own life? The truth stared me in the face, but my mind refused to accept it.

As I parked the car and stared at the vehicle that held Tommy's lifeless body, a wave of overwhelming anguish washed over me. It was too much to bear, so I sat in my seat, trying to gather the strength to face the reality that awaited me. The air around me felt thick with disbelief, as if the world itself couldn't comprehend the tragedy that had unfolded.

Entering the house, I could feel the presence of my baby brother. The memories of him flooded my senses, his scent lingering in the air. The sight of his belongings, all boxed up and tucked away, struck me as odd. It was as if he was not welcome or living there, as if his existence had been erased.

Making my way to the room where Tommy had taken his own life, I felt my legs give way beneath me. Collapsing to the floor, I clutched onto the shirt that had been removed from his body, desperate to hold onto something tangible, something that connected me to him. The cord that he had used to wrap around his neck seemed to taunt me, a painful reminder of the irreversible act that had stolen him away from us.

Tears streamed down my face as I fell to my knees, my voice cracking as I pleaded with God to wake me from this nightmare. The pain was unimaginable, the emptiness in my heart a void that could never be filled. How could I go on without my baby brother, without his infectious laughter and his unwavering love?

The days that followed blurred together, a haze of grief and disbelief. It felt as if I was floating through a fog, disconnected from the world around me. Each breath was a struggle, each moment a reminder of the gaping hole in my life. But amidst the pain, a search for answers began to gnaw at me. I needed to understand why Tommy had chosen this path, why he had kept his suffering hidden from us all.

As I ventured into his closet, a mix of confusion and raw emotions overwhelmed me. Why were his belongings boxed up, as if he had already left this world? It was a painful realization that perhaps this place he had called home had been a living hell for him. The weight of that realization only deepened my anguish, as I grappled with the guilt of not being there for him when he needed me most.

In the midst of my shattered reality, I clung to the memories of Tommy's love. I longed for him to know just how deeply he was missed, how much his absence had torn our family apart. The words "I love you" echoed in my mind, a bittersweet reminder of the love that would forever remain unspoken.

Though the truth of Tommy's pain was now undeniable, I found myself unable to fully comprehend it. The pieces of this tragic puzzle didn't fit together neatly, leaving me lost in a maze of unanswered questions. But deep down, I knew that I had to find a way to make sense of it all. In the face of unimaginable grief, I vowed to seek out the truth, to honor Tommy's memory by shedding light on the darkness that consumed him.

————

In the hotel room, days after his untimely demise, I found myself paralyzed with shock. The image of him hanging himself without a single goodbye haunted me, rendering me immobile.

Just as I was lost in my thoughts, the phone rang, and I hesitantly answered. It was my sister-in-law, Jenn, who asked me if I was aware that Tommy had a brain tumor. Apparently, the tumor had been growing for several years.

The news seemed surreal, and I had to pinch myself to confirm it wasn't a dream. Perhaps there was more to his actions than met the eye. Tommy's diagnosis shed light on his irrational behavior and inability to distinguish truth from fiction. This tumor in the frontal lobe had caused him to act out of character, even leading to his tragic decision to end his life. As devastating as it was, this revelation provided a glimmer of understanding amidst the darkness. We were now faced with the daunting task of making arrangements for his final farewell, all while navigating the restrictions imposed by the ongoing COVID-19 pandemic. The limitations on attendees and the need for virtual participation made the already challenging process even more difficult. Yet, we had no choice but to adhere to the rules. COVID-19 had affected everyone, and we had to adapt accordingly. Video conferencing platforms like Zoom became our means of connecting with loved ones during the funeral service, a bittersweet substitute for physical presence. Amidst the preparations and discussions surrounding this heartbreaking tragedy, tensions rose, and anger consumed some members of our family. Blame was thrown around, hurtful words were spoken, and irreversible damage was done. Witnessing the ugliness and mental sickness that surfaced in people during these trying times disgusted me to the core. How could we still be fighting and treating each other so terribly, even in the face of such immense grief? It felt as though I couldn't bear any more pain. The weight of it all made me question whether I even wanted to continue living. The survival guilt weighed heavily on me, and the loss of my loved ones to suicide and drug overdose left me feeling utterly alone. As my world crumbled like an avalanche, suffocating me, I struggled to find a way to move forward. The thought of becoming the fifth victim crossed my mind, but deep down, I knew I had to find the strength to overcome this darkness. While devastation surrounded me, I held onto the hope that by planting seeds of positivity and growth in others, I could make a difference in this world. However, in that moment, disbelief and despair were my constant companions.

## Seeking Relief

Navigating therapy during the COVID-19 pandemic was like trying to hike through a treacherous forest. Each step forward was met with obstacles and the weight of losing my siblings made the journey even more challenging. It felt like I was lost, unsure if I could ever find my way back to a sense of normalcy. However, my therapist became my guide, willingly venturing into the wilderness with me. Instead of placing her on a pedestal, I saw her as a compassionate companion who went above and beyond to meet me in nature, providing a safe space for me to process my grief. In this dark and confusing terrain, I struggled with illogical thoughts and survivor's guilt, questioning why I was still alive while my siblings were not. Recognizing that our shared experiences of childhood abuse had altered our brains, I faced the difficult task of owning the damage and seeking healing. It was through this journey that I discovered the importance of surrendering to the process, willing to try anything to find freedom and breathe again.

# First Summer Without Tommy

During the summer, my husband and I had the pleasure of hosting my nieces while their mother underwent surgery. We decided to have them participate in the TAECOLE summer camp program to keep them busy. Little did I know that these two weeks would be filled with extraordinary occurrences.

One day, as I sat by the duck pond at the botanical gardens, I noticed movement in the water. To my surprise, a turtle emerged and slowly made its way towards us. It was unusual since turtles typically shy away from people, but this one seemed different. It walked right up to my husband and me, its head out of the shell, as it stared at us intently. Time seemed to stand still during that moment, and I couldn't help but wonder if it was a sign from my baby brother, Tom. The encounter was so unexpected and profound, leaving me with a sense that he was trying to let us know that he was okay.

As the week progressed, more signs seemed to manifest. One day, a hawk landed right in front of our window, clutching a pigeon. It gazed directly at us, and I immediately felt a connection to Tom. Convinced that this was his way of communicating with us, I called out to my nieces. As they rushed downstairs, the hawk patiently waited for them, almost as if it recognized their presence. From that moment on, the hawk continued to visit us whenever thoughts of my brother filled my mind.

A few days later, my husband and nieces were driving during heavy rainfall and encountered a massive turtle in the middle of the road. Realizing it was in danger, they quickly rescued it and wrapped it in a blanket. My nieces held the turtle in our backseat while my husband drove it back to the botanical gardens, where it likely belonged. Yet again, another spirit animal crossed our path. Was it merely coincidence? I couldn't be sure, but the occurrences felt as if my brother Tommy was speaking to us, making his presence known.

With each encounter of these spirit animals throughout the weeks, it instilled a sense of peace within me. The coincidences provided a glimmer of hope, a belief that my brother had found his peace and final destination. Whether it was all coincidence or not, I chose to embrace the signs as messages from Tommy, assuring us that he was okay.

# Last Letter from Tommy
*July 23, 2020*

*Maggie, I'm so proud of you!!*

*Your courage never ceases to amaze me. It breaks my heart I left you alone there today.*

*Always know I love you and will visit our sister soon.*

*My heart is heavy today. Not only for our dear sister, but you as well.*

*Please don't take me not being with you all as a slight. I assure you that we all walk in each other's hearts always and forever! Thanks again for being so amazing. And although I've not said it enough to you... hear me now! I'm so very proud of you and all you have accomplished and all you have overcome!*

*Love always, your baby brother.*

*Keep being a hero. Love ya, sissy.*

# Last Note to Tommy
*February 12, 2023*

*My brother Tommy, I miss you more than the sun shines on a summer day, more than the leaves fall from the trees in autumn. I will love you always, and never forget the adventures we were meant to have together, like two birds soaring through the sky, experiencing the beauty of life. And just like those birds, we were supposed to build nests of memories, watch our children grow, and eventually become grandparents, cherishing every moment of our golden years. But now, as you rest in peace, I carry your love in my heart, and it will forever be etched in my soul. Until we meet again, my heart will ache with longing, but your spirit will guide me through the darkness, like a lighthouse guiding ships to safety.*

*-Maggie*

## A Visit from Tommy

As I stood there in the hotel room in Fishkill, NY, my heart pounding, I couldn't believe what I was seeing. It was as if time had stood still, and there was my brother Tommy, sitting at the edge of the bed. I couldn't tell if it was a dream or a vision, but I knew deep down that it was him.

Confused and overwhelmed, I quickly made my way to the bathroom, hoping that when I returned, Tommy would still be there. But to my astonishment, when I stepped back into the room, he was sitting on a chair, his legs draped over the edge, just as he used to do. His toothbrush and towel were casually hanging from his shoulder.

I couldn't contain my emotions any longer, and I blurted out, "Tom, what are you doing here? Why did you have to leave us like that?" Tears welled up in my eyes as I desperately sought answers.

Tom looked at me with a mixture of sadness and understanding. "I just had to go, Maggie," he said softly. "I couldn't take it anymore."

Confusion and frustration filled my mind as I pressed him further. "But why, Tommy? Why did you have to leave us like this?" I pleaded with him, hoping for some clarity.

With a heavy sigh, Tommy replied, "It wasn't just about me, Maggie. It was about something that happened. Something Joan Alice wrote. It was too much for me to handle. Jen saw it too, and they just wouldn't let it go. I couldn't bear the weight of it anymore."

I was taken aback by his words. How could something on social media have such a profound impact on him? But my focus remained on the question that haunted me the most. "But why did you have to leave the way you did, Tommy? Why couldn't you say something, reach out to us?"

Tommy's gaze met mine, and I could sense the pain in his eyes. "Mags, it's not all about you," he said, his voice tinged with frustration. His words stung, but I knew deep down he was right. There were things I couldn't fully understand or comprehend.

Feeling a mix of emotions, I retreated to the bathroom once again, trying to process everything that had transpired. But as I emerged, ready to confront Tommy once more, he was gone. Panic surged through my veins, and I raced downstairs, my tears blurring my vision.

I found myself on a dirt road, chasing after him. "Tommy, please don't leave me!" I cried out, my voice filled with desperation. But he turned towards me, a look of sadness on his face.

"I have to go back there," he said, his voice barely audible. "They want to take me back."

As I looked past him, I saw a towering presence, faceless yet overwhelming. It stood beside him, a silent witness to our exchange. And as my gaze followed its direction, I saw a graveyard, a solemn reminder of the finality of death.

Collapsing to my knees, I couldn't hold back my tears any longer. "Please, Tommy, don't leave me like this," I sobbed. But as I looked up, he was gone. It became clear to me that it was not a physical presence but a spiritual visitation.

In that moment, I understood that Tommy had come to me in that hotel room to offer some form of closure, to let me know that he was at peace. It was a bittersweet encounter, filled with longing and sorrow, but also a glimmer of solace.

His visitation reminded me that love transcends the boundaries of life and death. Though Tommy was no longer physically present, his spirit lived on, forever etched in my heart. And from that day forward, I carried his memory with me, finding comfort in the signs and whispers that reminded me of his enduring love.

CHAPTER FIVE

# The Enemy Within

## Healing

As I sat there, recounting the painful memories of my past, I realized that I had spent years running away from my own truth. The trauma of my upbringing had shaped me in ways I couldn't fully comprehend. But now, with the news of Danny's passing, it was as if the weight of all those unresolved emotions came crashing down on me.

I looked at my husband, Ray, who had always been my rock, and saw the concern etched on his face. He knew the struggles I had faced with my family but had always been there to support me. In that moment, I realized that I couldn't continue to bury my pain and pretend that everything was okay. I needed to confront my past head-on and find a way to heal, breath.

The days that followed were a blur of grief and introspection. I began to unravel the complexities of my history: the abuse Danny and I had endured in the Gasparino's home and the lasting impact it had on our lives. I couldn't change the past, but I could find healing and redemption.

I sought Trauma therapy, finally opening up about the deep wounds that had haunted me for so long. My therapist helped me understand that I wasn't defined by the actions of my family members, including Danny. I had the power to break the cycle of abuse and create a different path for myself.

As I delved into the process of healing, I realized that forgiveness was a crucial step in my journey. It wasn't about condoning the actions of those who had hurt me, but rather releasing the anger and resentment that had consumed me for so long. Forgiveness wasn't for them; it was for me, a way to let go and find peace within myself.

In the months that followed, I began to rebuild my life. I surrounded myself with a supportive network of friends who understood the complexities of my past. Together, we created a chosen family that provided the love and acceptance I had always longed for.

Although the scars of my past would always be a part of me, I refused to let them define me. I dedicated myself to personal growth, embracing my individuality, and finding joy in the present moment. It was a continuous journey, but one that I was determined to navigate with grace and resilience.

With time, I started to rebuild bridges with some of my siblings who were also seeking their own paths to healing. We acknowledged the pain we had caused one another and slowly began to mend the fractured relationships. It wasn't easy, but we were committed to breaking the cycle of dysfunction and creating a new legacy for future generations.

As I reflect on my journey, I realize that the pain and hardship I experienced have shaped me into the person I am today. I am no longer defined by the brokenness of my past but rather empowered by the strength I found within myself to overcome it.

Through the darkness, I discovered the power of resilience, the beauty of forgiveness, and the importance of self-love. My twin brother may no longer be physically present, but his memory serves as a constant reminder of the fragility of life and the urgency to live authentically and with purpose.

I now know that healing is not a linear process; it's messy and unpredictable. But I am committed to embracing every step, knowing that each day brings me closer to wholeness and a brighter future. And as I continue to heal, I will honor Danny's memory by living a life filled with compassion, authenticity, and a deep appreciation for the resilience of the human spirit.

Thoughts of why:

It's like walking on a tightrope, carefully balancing my emotions and trying to find stability in the midst of chaos. Just as I start to regain my footing, another blow comes crashing down, shattering my heart into a thousand pieces. It's as if I am caught in a relentless storm, tossed around by the winds of tragedy. Each loss feels like a heavy weight pressing down on my soul, leaving me breathless and broken. Like a cruel game of dominos, the people I hold dear are falling one by one, leaving me bewildered and questioning the unfairness of it all. The pain is so overwhelming that it brings me to my knees, unable to comprehend the magnitude of grief and loss that I am forced to endure.

## My Reflection
*2023*

Imagine being lost at sea, desperately trying to stay afloat as the waves crash around you. In this turbulent struggle, you find yourself clinging onto a raft that represents the reasons for living - the moments, experiences, and people that give you hope and purpose. However, there are times when the darkness and despair threaten to overwhelm you, pulling you down into the depths. It's like sinking deeper into the water, feeling exhausted and twisted by anger and sadness. You desperately yearn for a sign, a lifebuoy or some kind of support to rescue you from drowning in the overwhelming emotions.

## Shipwrecked: A Poem for Tommy

*The pain of losing you is like a ship sinking in the darkest depths of the ocean. I wish I had known the weight of your suffering and been able to offer support like a lighthouse guiding a lost vessel. But now, all I have are memories, unable to change the past. The void you left behind is immeasurable, and I long for your presence, dear baby brother. My love for you ran as deep as the ocean, but I regret that we never had the chance to bid farewell.*

# CHAPTER SIX

# Crossing Over

Never in my wildest dreams could I have imagined waking up and finding myself on this side of the tracks, the side that is often met with torment and judgment. Here I am, on the North Shore, the Gold Coast of Long Island, New York. Everything feels unfamiliar to me—the way people live, dress, and even smell. I used to worry about crossing over to this side, fearing that once you do, there's no going back. But the reality couldn't be further from the truth.

It's not about what you wear or where you come from. It's about the essence we carry within us, the experiences that shape us. Our roots mold us into the people we are today. It doesn't mean we have to remain stuck in the past, drowning in addiction, illness, or suffering. But there will always be a part of us that remembers our origins and the lessons learned. For me, it's the ability to read people in an instant. Growing up on the other side of the tracks taught me the survival skill of quickly assessing others, anticipating what might happen next. It's a skill I honed out of necessity, a means of navigating an uncertain world.

Yet, in my pursuit of reaching the next level, I sometimes find myself questioning how I got here. It's as if I need to pinch myself to believe it's not just a dream. The imposter syndrome creeps in, accompanied by survivor's guilt. People often talk about being on the wrong side of the tracks and feeling out of place, but it's more than just a figure of speech—it's a real struggle. And it's tough.

But I refuse to succumb to a life of numbness, drowning my emotions in substances or pretending to be someone I'm not. I choose to be fully awake and present in my journey. This chapter is about sharing that struggle, reminding others that they are not alone in their feelings of worthlessness and self-doubt. It's a universal experience shared by anyone who has risen from nothing to achieve success in their chosen field. We all question our place in the world and whether we truly deserve to be where we are. It's a delicate balance of acknowledging our accomplishments without allowing the ego or the temptations of the seven deadly sins to consume us: pride, greed, lust, envy, gluttony, wrath and sloth.

So, the next time someone remarks, "You're from the other side of the tracks," pause and reflect on the deeper meaning behind those words. It's a statement that carries weight and can be hurtful beyond what most people can comprehend. Embrace it and say, "Yes, I was born on the other side of the tracks, and now I live on both sides." There is good and bad on both sides, but it manifests differently. Bad people exist everywhere, regardless of social status. Greed, sickness, and cruelty know no boundaries. It's just that some individuals have been exposed to better education and opportunities, enabling them to make more informed choices. When someone knows better but still engages in wrongdoing, the impact is even greater.

I am a product of both sides of the tracks, navigating the complexities of life. So, let us not judge or make assumptions based on where someone comes from. We are all capable of growth, change, and redemption. The tracks that divide us are merely physical representations of the barriers we create in our minds. It's time to break free from those constraints and embrace the shared humanity that unites us all.

## Goodbye, Tragic Past

Flashback (PTSD): The bursts arrive abruptly, catching me off guard. I am transported back to my childhood, a vulnerable and innocent state. In a desperate attempt to escape, I take a deep breath, hoping for a reprieve.

But this time, I am fully aware. I can feel every touch, every sting. It's as if the pain has become tangible, impossible to ignore. With trembling lips, I utter a plea to God, begging for a momentary release.

Sweat trickles down my forehead, but I dare not make a single movement, or even breathe. I'm afraid that the slightest sound or motion will invite more suffering. In this twisted slumber, I am neither asleep nor awake.

I know that the next time will be quicker, more merciless. I must prepare myself, refine my timing. The strength within me is waning, and I feel like a broken crayon, disintegrating and struggling to remain within the confines of the lines.

Exhausted, I lie there, praying for the absence of anyone else. I cannot bear the weight of another presence upon me, invading me. The pain is unbearable, the sting insufferable. Am I exaggerating? No, this is my truth, a chapter in my life that spans only a few years.

Despite the anguish, I am grateful to God. For He has granted me the ability to feel, to experience the depths of hatred, longing, and pain unlike any other. I offer my soul, my heart, my desires as gratitude for the blessings bestowed upon me.

Now, I wait. Unsure if it will be hell or heaven that awaits me. But I hold onto the belief that it will be better than this torment. You, God, assured me of this when you left me awake to witness, to feel, to shiver in agony.

Thank you, God, for making me unique, for choosing only a select few to understand both heaven and hell.

# CHAPTER SEVEN

# Gerri "Mother"

Mother Cole
Year 2000-ish

## Mother's Passing
*February 16, 2023*

Around Noon, I received a call from my sister Joan. She informed

me that our mother, Geraldine Cole, had only a few hours to live.

Despite her age of 86 and my previous anticipation of her passing, I couldn't help but feel hopeful that she would pull through, just as she had in the past. Though she was ill and frail, she was a strong woman who had survived a car crash and internal injuries. As I drove to be by her side, I prayed she wouldn't leave this world before I arrived.

Upon entering her room, I knew that this time was different. The nurse's sorrowful expressions and the sound of my mother's labored breathing confirmed my fears. Despite the anger and pain my mother had caused me in the past, I couldn't help but feel sorry for her. What kind of life had led her to this point? As I sat by her side, I thought of all the times I had avoided visiting her, but now it was too late.

My brother Tiny called to say goodbye to our mother, and his words broke my heart. He apologized for things he had and hadn't done and told her she could be with our father and siblings who had passed away before her. As soon as we hung up, my mother's breathing changed again. The nurse confirmed that it wouldn't be long now, and within minutes, my mother had taken her last breath.

I fell apart as I realized that she was really gone. Despite my distorted reality and the inability to comprehend the moment, I knew she had left this Earth. My nephew Brocki arrived just in time to offer his condolences, but nothing could ease the pain of losing what never was and never will be.

## The Back Story of Gerri

Born November 24, 1932, in the Hudson Valley in upstate New York to Robert and Margaret Downs, Gerri's story is a painful and tragic one. She was born into poverty and addiction, with her father being a drunk who didn't care for holding a job. Her mother, Margaret, eventually threw him out and sent Gerri and her brother Sonny to live with their aunt and uncle.

Unfortunately, their uncle was a man of rage and law enforcement, which gave him the privilege of doing whatever he wanted without being held accountable. He would beat his wife and sadistically torment Gerri and Sonny, treating them like animals. The worst night came when he beat his pregnant wife, Mary, causing her death after giving birth. Gerri would hide her aunt's bloodied clothes under her bed, a haunting reminder of the tragedy.

After being homeless for some time, Benny, their mother's boyfriend, agreed to take Gerri in, being that she was the older of the two. However, Sonny was left to fend for himself on the streets, eventually ending up in juvenile detention and later prison. The lack of guidance and love in his life led him down a dark path of abuse and torment towards others.

Gerri eventually returned home with her mother, Margaret, however, she would soon experience abuse from Benny during the nights as she slept between her mother and Benny. Despite the hardships, Gerri became the main breadwinner in the household, working hard to support herself and her mother.

It was during this time that she met my father, Lee, who was significantly older than her. She hoped he would be the man to rescue her from her troubled life and give her the love and stability she craved. However, Lee turned out to be a disappointment, cheating and lying, causing her more heartache.

Despite all the hardships she faced, Gerri went on to have 11 children. Rumors suggest that some of us may have been fathered by other men, which wouldn't be surprising given the circumstances.

Reflecting on my mother's life, I can't help but see the demented nature of her actions and the pain she caused her children. However, I also wonder what she went through that led her to become the person she was. I know some of the stories that she'd shared, but I'm sure there is so much more that she has never told us.

Throughout the years, I distanced myself from my mother in order to protect my own sanity and personal growth. There were times when she begged me to see her, claiming she was dying, but she had always been dying in one way or another. Her stories of illness and suffering became too much for me to handle.

If you find yourself in a similar situation with a parent who is detrimental to your mental stability, it's important to prioritize your own well-being. I made the difficult decision to save myself, and I am grateful for where I am today. Despite the pain and hardships, everything I've experienced has shaped me into the person I am, allowing me to empathize and connect with others on a deep level.

Although my mother may not have given me much, she did give me the gift of reading people and understanding them within seconds. Through therapy and self-help, I've come to embrace this gift as my superpower, not judging it but using it to reach others. For that, I am thankful to Geraldine Downes Cole, my mother. I can only hope that she is in a better place now, free from the disconnect of the reality that plagued her. Perhaps one day, we will meet again, and she will be at peace.

# Guilt of A Survivor

In the depths of my heart, a void does reside,

A darkness that engulfs, where guilt does reside.

For I, a survivor, left you behind,

In a world so cruel, so unkind.

In '81, I found my escape,

Leaving you, my dear sister, in a painful landscape.

How could I not shield you from the abusers' toll?

I carry the weight of this guilt, an unbearable load.

Oh, Danny boy, I offer my deepest apology,

For failing to provide you with empathy.

Blinded by anger, my heart turned cold,

While you suffered, feeling helpless and controlled.

Tommy, you battled a tumor unseen,

Unstable ground beneath you, a life so mean.

Now I must navigate a world without the stories we once preserved.

The absence of you three, a void hard to bear,

In sorrow's embrace, I search for solace and repair.

No words can express the ache in my core,

*But I vow to honor your memory forevermore.*

*In this journey of healing, I'll carry your light,*

*Seeking forgiveness, embracing what's right.*

*Though guilt may haunt, I'll strive to find peace,*

*And ensure your love and legacy never cease.*

*For in the depths of my heart, your spirits reside,*

*Guiding me forward, with love as my guide.*

*I'll honor your lives, each and every day,*

*And in my heart, your memories will forever stay.*

*-Maggie Messina*

*December, 2023*

## CHAPTER EIGHT

# *Father*

L-R: Dad, Uncle Edward and Great Mummy (1930s), Maggs and Dad
(1975)

*The curse that was believed to be plagued on our family early on in Gerritsen Beach Brooklyn, NY in the 1930's continues to wreak havoc today.*

In the depths of my family history lies the enigma that was Lee Roy Cole Jr, my father. Born June 22, 1922, in New York. He possessed strong Protestant beliefs and took pride in his English heritage. However, beneath his seemingly virtuous exterior, he harbored a deep well of prejudice that tainted his character. Growing up in the era of segregation and enduring the hardships of the Great Depression, he was shaped by his experiences. Tragically, his father, a skilled sniper in the US Army, lost his sight in a devastating accident, leading to his retirement from service.

The devastating loss of my beloved Uncle Edward, Granddad's pride and joy, sent shockwaves through our family. His tragic demise, falling to his death in front of a subway train in New York City, remains shrouded in mystery. Rumors swirled, suggesting he either fell or took his own life upon returning from war, his spirit forever altered. Gripped by debilitating headaches and consumed by depression, he struggled to reclaim the life he left behind. The controversy surrounding his demise left my grandfather broken, driving him to drown his sorrows in an increasingly heavy reliance on alcohol.

The weight of this tragedy pushed my grandfather further into the abyss, confining him to his room while he sought solace in the bottle. Prior to this heart-wrenching event, he struggled to find steady employment, leading his family on a nomadic journey from one place to another. Often finding shelter in rooms above or behind bars, it seemed as though fate had a cruel sense of irony when my father later found himself in a similar situation, residing above a bar and succumbing to his own battle with alcohol.

These abhorrent values of prejudice and anger were passed down to my siblings, but I refused to let them take root in my heart. I vividly recall a moment during my teenage years when my father and I boarded a bus together. His eyes fixated on a group of carefree children playfully jumping around at the back of the bus, he spewed venomous words, referring to them as "animals" who belonged in a zoo. A man, visibly enraged by this display of bigotry, confronted my father with threatening gestures. Fear gripped my heart, fearing for our safety, but my father stood his ground, goading the man further. Eventually, the man realized my father was merely a deranged old, white man, prompting him to walk away. In that pivotal moment, I made a solemn vow to myself never to harbor such hatred and ugliness within me. I resolved to find beauty in every soul, regardless of their skin color or background, shaping the way I would forge connections and relationships in the years to come.

It is crucial to acknowledge the troubled upbringing my father himself endured. Significantly older than my mother, their relationship always carried an unsettling aura of predation and impropriety. They crossed paths when she was just a teenager, and their union left me feeling uneasy. Pregnancy came swiftly after their marriage, and my father's presence in our lives became sporadic, leaving my mother to bear the burden of raising us alone. This pattern persisted, with my mother eventually turning to the solace of alcohol and relying on the kindness of others to care for us. Throughout it all, my father was idolized by many, while my mother bore the weight of blame for his absence.

As I reflect upon the tumultuous journey of my own life and the web of lies my father spun, I am acutely aware of the profound impact his prejudices had on me. However, rather than succumbing to bitterness, I am grateful for the invaluable lessons I derived from his actions. They ignited within me a relentless pursuit of understanding and compassion for others. I forged incredible friendships with individuals hailing from diverse backgrounds, breaking free from the privileged norms my father upheld. Although a sense of repulsion lingers when I think of him, I also yearn for his happiness and peace in the afterlife. The revelation of our Irish heritage, unearthed through DNA testing after his passing, further emphasized the irony of his hateful beliefs. I find myself questioning the origins of these falsehoods, but I comprehend that societal pressures and the era he grew up in may have molded his choices.

Ultimately, my heart now overflows with empathy for my mother, recognizing that she never stood a chance in life. Manipulated by my father and taken advantage of from a tender age, she endured unimaginable hardships. I am left to ponder how her life might have unfolded had she been given the opportunity to grow and mature before entangling herself in such a toxic relationship. The predatory nature of their dynamic and the toll it exacted on her soul have become clear to me.

As I navigate the labyrinthine path of life, I strive to remember that judging others solely based on their skin color or background is not only unjust but also hampers the experience of having extraordinary, diverse connections and relationships.

# CHAPTER 9

# In Session: Grasping The Truth About Danny

I learned certain truths about Danny before he passed, and the situation made me incredibly sick. I can't believe it took me so long to fully grasp the severity of who Danny had become, but now I do, and it's overwhelming. I never connected the dots before, but it's clear that he's been reenacting the horrors we experienced. It makes me physically ill and leaves me with this empty feeling whenever it comes to mind. The level of sickness is almost unbearable, and it has forever altered how I view twins. It has shattered a significant part of who I am.

I can't help but wonder if Danny saw it as some twisted reward when he would do those despicable things to us as children, and even now. In some messed up way, I feel implicated, guilty, even though I know it doesn't make any logical sense. But these emotions are real and present. It's deeply disturbing to me. It's like I've reached a point where there are no more secrets to keep if I want to escape from this darkness. But it's unbelievably difficult. It feels like no matter how bad things were in the past, they just keep getting darker. Have they always been this bad, and am I only now fully awake to it?

And the fact that he actually confessed to Ted, deriving pleasure from sharing it and Ted acknowledging it… it changes everything. It makes everything undeniably real and exposed. I've spent so much time and energy denying it, hoping that it would somehow disappear. But now I have to face the truth, and it's seriously affecting me and disturbing me to my core. The level of sadism, sexual enjoyment, evil, cruelty, and abuse… it's a lot to process.

I don't even know how to begin processing it all. Dr. Rob continuously reminds me that, "Sweetie, you're doing it now." But it's just extremely challenging to accept that I had such a twisted twin. How does anyone come to terms with such disgust? How do I make these vivid flashbacks and haunting dreams stop?

This is truly disturbing me. Seeing it on TV news and reading about it in the papers is bad enough, but the fact that I actually lived through it... it's almost too much to bear.

## The Only Way to Freedom is Through the Pain

Dr. Rob continues to reiterate in every therapy session that the only way to heal from the pain is to face it head-on. It can be frustrating to hear the same message repeatedly, and sometimes I just want to forget everything and move on. After years of processing and enduring intense emotional turmoil, there comes a moment when something clicks, and I suddenly begin to understand what Dr. Rob has been trying to teach me.

I realize that I can't continue running away from the truth and burying the secrets deep within me. Suppressing them only leads to physical and emotional illnesses like cancer and heart disease. Although there are times when it feels like succumbing to these illnesses might be easier than facing the truth, I make the decision to dive into the depths of my pain and confront it head-on. It's like plunging into water, allowing it to engulf me as I embrace the truth.

This journey is far from easy. There are no sessions where we laugh and joyfully hand over our payment, ecstatic to be there. It's hard work, but it's necessary. It's the most challenging thing I've ever done, but I know deep down that I want to be free and experience true happiness. I want to break free from the chains of my past, and I'm willing to do whatever it takes to achieve that.

So, I continue to take the plunge, diving headfirst into every aspect of my pain and trauma. I spend the next several years dedicated to this process, knowing that it is the path towards freedom and happiness. It's not an easy journey, but I believe that in the end, it will all be worth it... letting go of the anger that has "protected" me.

I soon came to realize that anger has become a significant part of my identity. I have held onto that anger tightly, as if it were a hot cup of coffee in the morning, providing me with some semblance of protection. However, I've begun to understand that this anger was slowly killing me. It kept others at a distance and prevented me from truly experiencing and processing my emotions.

There came a point in my journey with Dr. Rob where I realized that in order to truly live, accept myself, and experience love, I had to let go of this anger. This is/was one of the most challenging steps I had to take because it meant becoming vulnerable, something I had always feared due to the possibility of being hurt or rejected. But with Dr. Rob's guidance, I decided it was time to give it a try.

I gradually started to let go of the anger and allowed myself to feel the emotions that lay beneath it, no matter how scary and debilitating they were. I learned that the only way to move forward was to fully experience and process these feelings. It was a difficult and painful journey, but it was the path to freedom.

Growing up, I witnessed and experienced things that no one should ever have to go through. Tragically, I lost four of my siblings along the way. Whether it was through suicide, fentanyl overdoses, or the consequences of my mother's drinking and drug use during pregnancy, they were all gone. I found myself alone, grappling with the guilt of surviving while they did not.

It was strange to think back to the times when Dr. Rob would mention that tragedy was coming my way. I used to dismiss it, thinking that nothing could be worse than what I had already experienced. But then my siblings started to take their own lives, and the full weight of pain, agony, and loneliness brought me to my knees. I began to question why I was still here and why they weren't. What made me so special? I even contemplated joining them, believing that perhaps it would be easier.

But then I thought about the people in my life, the ones who relied on me, the ones I had mentored and taught. They were like the customers in an ice cream shop, eagerly awaiting my presence. I couldn't bear to disappoint them. This realization led me to think outside the box and consider if there was some form of trauma treatment that could help me release the pain and nightmares that haunted me.

That's when I discovered Noelle Damon, LCSW-R DAAETS, RYT, and her various trauma treatments. At first, it sounded crazy to me, and I didn't believe it would work. But when you're desperate enough, you're willing to try anything.

So, I took a leap of faith and embarked on this new form of treatment, hoping that it would bring some relief from the pain I carried within me.

## Trauma Treatment

Trusting this journey meant enduring unimaginable hardships, but it also brought forth personal growth and transformation. Despite the challenges, I continued to push forward, determined to overcome the obstacles that life threw my way. The path ahead was uncertain, but I held onto the belief that trusting the process would ultimately lead me to a place of healing and peace.

EMDR therapy with Noelle was a scary and uncertain journey for me. I did my research before starting the treatment and understood that it was a treatment to help with severe PTSD, but I still didn't know what to expect.

The news of my twin brother Danny's overdose and passing added another layer of pain and trauma to my life. I had always used dissociation as a coping mechanism, but now I had to confront the deep-rooted emotions that I had been avoiding.

Meeting Noelle in person, I felt like I was floating on another planet. The flood of memories and emotions was overwhelming, and I questioned if I would ever be able to survive this ordeal. But I kept moving forward, putting one foot in front of the other, and praying for strength.

The EMDR sessions with Noelle were exhausting. The various techniques used, such as lights, rapid eye movement, and tapping, were all part of the healing process. There were moments when I wanted to give up, when the emotions became too intense to bear. But I persevered, unraveling the layers of trauma over months and even years.

The tragic loss of my siblings, one after another, has left a deep and indelible mark on my heart. The loss of my brother was devastating, and it shook our family to its core, especially my little sister Alice. Just as we were trying to cope with that immense pain, another tragedy struck with the untimely loss of Alice. The weight of grief seemed unbearable, and I found myself shattered once again.

To my disbelief, the cycle of heartbreak continued when, seven months later, my baby brother Tommy also took his life. The revelation of an undiagnosed brain tumor, due to the lack of testing during the COVID-19 pandemic, added a layer of complexity to our already profound sorrow. It felt like a relentless onslaught of tragedy and loss, testing the limits of my strength and resilience.

Amidst the darkness, I clung to the hope that Trauma /EMDR therapy would provide me with the tools and resilience needed to navigate this overwhelming grief. In the midst of such profound sorrow, I hold on to the memories of my siblings and the love we shared, hoping to find solace and healing in the midst of this unfathomable loss.

Throughout my Trauma/EMDR treatment with Noelle, I felt buried under an avalanche of pain and grief. Noelle even questioned if I felt I needed more than she could offer, but I continued to proceed forward. I felt angry and alone, abandoned by my loved ones. But through the therapy sessions, I slowly found my way to the other side.

I realized that my purpose in life was not just about myself, but about being a survivor for others who have experienced similar pain. No one understands the depths of despair and the scars left behind like someone who has been through it themselves. Trauma and talk therapy were effective, lifesaving tools, but the real work came from within me. I had to accept that there is no magic pill, it was all me.

I am forever grateful to those who never gave up on me, who refused to let me give up on myself. Trauma treatment and therapy have shown me that healing is possible, and now my purpose is to support others who are trapped in their own anguish.

## Unraveling the Shadows

I remember when I was young and hungry – hungry for love, food, and attention. As a child, my siblings and I did our best to survive in our own personal hell. Singing songs and rocking away the pain became our escape from the chaos that surrounded us. We knew that if anyone discovered the pain we were hiding, we could be taken away again. We couldn't go back to those who had broken us back when.

So, we stayed silent and stuck together. No one dared to mess with us. We were as close as family could be. But I've come to realize that unless someone has experienced the torture and hunger of poverty and mentally ill parents, they will never truly understand the torment we went through. It was a road we had to travel to survive.

The effects of mental, sexual, and physical abuse left scars that run deeper than most can comprehend. We may try to form relationships and seek love, but deep down, we know that we have been forever changed. Our way of feeling and thinking had been rewired.

Unwiring the damage done takes an incredible amount of strength and determination. It is a monumental task for someone who has come from brokenness to learn how to trust, to believe in love, and to heal from the wounds of the past. It requires perseverance to break free from the cycle of abuse and rebuild a life filled with hope and happiness.

For years, I carried the weight of our traumatic childhood on my shoulders without fully understanding its impact. I carried both visible and invisible scars, struggling to navigate through life. But as I grew older, I realized that I couldn't continue living in the shadows of my past. I deserved better.

With the support of others, I embarked on a journey of self-discovery and healing. Therapy became my lifeline, a safe space where I could unravel the tangled mess of emotions that had been suppressed for far too long. It was there that I learned to identify the unhealthy patterns ingrained in me and gradually dismantle them.

Let me tell you, rewiring a damaged mind is no easy task. It requires countless hours of introspection and facing our deepest fears and insecurities head-on. It means allowing ourselves to be vulnerable, even when every instinct tells us to shut down and protect ourselves. It means learning to forgive, not just those who hurt us, but also ourselves for the years of self-blame and shame.

Through it all, I discovered the power of resilience. I learned that despite the darkness that once consumed me, there is a spark of light within each of us that can never be extinguished. I found solace in shared experiences, knowing that I was not alone in my struggles.

And slowly, ever so slowly, I began to rebuild. I formed new relationships based on trust and respect. I found the strength to love again, not just others, but myself as well. I embraced my scars as symbols of triumph over adversity, reminders of the strength that resides within me.

Yes, the journey was long and challenging, but it was worth it. I will always carry traces of the painful past, but I have also emerged stronger, wiser, and more compassionate than ever before. I have learned to find beauty in the brokenness and to use my experiences to uplift others who may be trapped in their own personal hells.

So, to anyone who has experienced the darkness of abuse and poverty, know that you are not alone. You have the capacity to heal, to rewrite your story, and to find happiness. It may be the most difficult thing you'll ever do, but the rewards are immeasurable. You deserve love, happiness, and a life free from the torment that once held you captive.

Keep fighting, keep believing, and never give up. You are stronger than you know, and your future holds endless possibilities for a life filled with joy and purpose.

# CHAPTER 10

# The Truth About Mary

Born on January 4th, 1966, my sister Mary's life was a constant reminder of the pain and suffering that can be inflicted upon innocent souls. Despite her numerous handicaps, she possessed a remarkable ability to communicate and understand through her senses of touch and smell. Mary knew and recognized each of us, her siblings, and we cherished the moments when she acknowledged our presence.

Unfortunately, Mary's life was far from easy. She endured unimaginable suffering, which I choose not to delve into for the sake of our own sanity. I have documented the details in my first book, *Making Maggie: Little Miss Tri-County,* for those who wish to know more. One thing became painfully clear to us over the years: Mary's struggles were not ours to bear. They were the burden of our parents, who failed to provide her with the care and love she deserved.

As children ourselves, it was incredibly challenging to care for Mary. We lacked the means to meet her basic needs, such as clean diapers, warm clothing, and proper nourishment. It was a haunting reality that haunted us for the rest of our lives. However, we eventually came to the realization that it was not our responsibility to carry the weight of our parent's sins. Mary's well-being was their responsibility, not ours.

One fateful day, Mary experienced a seizure that landed her in the hospital. My sister Alice, who had been caring for Mary, reached her breaking point. She turned to our father and expressed that she could no longer continue this exhausting journey. Alice bravely declared that we would no longer care for Mary at home. This decision changed everything and set in motion a series of events that would forever alter our lives.

Mary became a ward of the state, finally receiving the care and attention she deserved. Visiting her throughout the years was difficult, as it brought back painful memories of our shared past. While Mary wore her scars on the outside, we carried ours deep within us. She served as a constant reminder of the hardships we had endured together.

Tragically, Mary's journey came to an end on February 9, 2009. She suffered a seizure that led to aspiration, and she did not recover. I remember that day vividly, as it marked a pivotal moment in my life. It was the moment I realized that Mary, despite her challenges, was finally free from suffering. My sister Alice and I had the opportunity to care for her in her final days at the hospital, providing her with the love and attention she should have received throughout her life.

The only difficulty was that our mother, who had returned from yet another stint in rehab, was present in the room. It was a painful reminder of her neglect and the abuse Mary had endured under her care. Despite this, I choose to see it as a healing moment for us. We were able to do what was right for Mary, even in the presence of the one person who had failed her the most.

Mary's funeral was filled with raw emotions, and many people came to pay their respects. However, our mother was noticeably absent. At first, I was disturbed by her absence, but as time passed, I understood why she chose not to be there. Her presence would have only brought forth hurtful and cruel words from her children and the people who have spent the last decade caring for Mary, and she likely knew that. The pain in the room was palpable, like a heavy cloud hanging over us all.

Reflecting on Mary's life, I can confidently say that she was an angel among us. If anyone deserves to be called a saint, it is my sweet sister Mary. She was born into a world of torment and suffering, yet she managed to touch our lives in ways we could never have imagined. In her final days, she became a symbol of our pain and represented the resilience of the human spirit.

Mary, I loved you deeply, and I am grateful that you are now at peace. Your presence in my life has inspired me to dedicate myself to helping others who suffer at the hands of neglect and abuse. I will strive to make a difference and ensure that no child has to endure the pain that you experienced. We must remember that the choices we make during pregnancy have a profound impact on the lives of our children, both physically and emotionally. Let us not be selfish but instead do what is right for the precious lives growing within us.

# CHAPTER 11

# I Am Not Broken

To my beloved readers,

I stand before you at the end of a tumultuous journey, a journey filled with hardships, challenges, and moments of despair. But through unwavering determination and resilience, I have emerged from the depths of darkness and found a newfound freedom from the pain and abuse that once consumed me. Life has a way of throwing us off balance, making us question the very core of our humanity and our faith in something greater. The atrocities, the anger, and the ugliness that exist in the world can be overwhelming, leaving us disheartened at times.

Yet, I have come to understand that without experiencing suffering firsthand, we cannot truly comprehend the struggles of others. It is through our own pain that we acquire empathy and compassion for those who are currently enduring their own battles. Though I may sometimes lament the missed opportunities and the lack of love and support I experienced in my early years, I have come to realize that those experiences have shaped my purpose and my journey.

I understand that my book may be a challenging read, as it delves into the depths of my past. However, it is crucial to remember that it does not define who I am, nor does it define any of us as individuals. It serves as a testament to the strength and resilience of the human spirit. Despite the suffering we endure, it is the person we become that truly matters.

Each and every one of us carries a story within, waiting to be told. The question is, what are you willing to do to break the cycle of pain and become the catalyst for change that the world so desperately needs? I implore you to delve deep within your soul and embrace the power that resides within you. If you choose to embark on this journey of healing, staying true to your path no matter how arduous, the rewards will be immeasurable. You possess the ability to become the change the world yearns for, and I say this with utmost sincerity and conviction.

So, to all my readers, I encourage you to press forward, never losing sight of your inner strength, and always remembering that it is the person we become, despite the hardships we face, that defines us. Let us all strive to be the shining beacon of hope and transformation that the world so desperately craves.

In the final chapter of my book, I reflect upon the journey I have undertaken, filled with ups and downs, triumphs and heartaches. Over the past few years, I have dedicated myself to rebuilding my life and becoming a better person. It has not been an easy path, as I have encountered individuals who take pleasure in causing harm to others, be it physical or emotional. The discovery of this dark reality has been disheartening and heartbreaking.

However, I refuse to let the negativity of these individuals deter me from my mission to make the world a better place. While my story may be unique, I acknowledge that there are countless others who have suffered and endured hardships. Life has a way of knocking us down, sometimes burying us beneath the weight of our struggles. But in those moments of despair, there is always a glimmer of hope, a kind soul reaching out to lift us up.

When we find ourselves in that dark place, it is crucial to acknowledge our pain and sit with it. It may be overwhelming and debilitating, but we must remember that life goes on. Each of us faces our own challenges, and I have come to understand that pain is pain, regardless of its magnitude. We should never compare our pain to that of others, for suffering cannot be measured. Instead, we must summon the strength to rise again, refusing to remain on our knees when life knocks us down.

Yet, I must admit that this journey is remarkably challenging. The daily struggles, coupled with the unkindness of others, can make us question our purpose and the meaning behind it all. It becomes disheartening when we realize that justice is often absent in the world. However, in the face of such injustice, we must create our own sense of justice, living according to our own principles and doing what we know to be right.

To anyone reading this book, I urge you to discover your reason for living, that one thing that brings you joy and ignites your passion. Embrace your mission and continue moving forward, refusing to let jealousy and negativity hinder your growth. My own journey in this complicated and sometimes dark life has taught me that resilience is the key. People often ask me how I keep going, how I find the strength to face each new day despite the hardships. My answer is simple: "Fake it till you make it." Sometimes, we must pretend to be strong until we genuinely become strong. The reward is undeniably worth the effort.

In this unpredictable life, there are no guarantees. We cannot foresee what tomorrow holds or what it may take from us. However, we can control how we live our lives in the present, and the memories we create.

*BE TRUE! STAY YOU!*
*YOU ARE YOUR GREATEST SUPERPOWER.*

Maggie Messina

# EMDR INFORMATION AND HELPFUL LINKS

If you are suffering from trauma, EMDR therapy may be a valuable tool to help you on your journey to healing.

## Excerpt from EMDR: The Breakthrough Therapy for Anxiety, Stress and Trauma

After the therapist and client agree that EMDR therapy is a good fit, the beginning sessions will involve discussing what the client wants to work on and improving the client's ability to manage distress.

When ready for the next phases of EMDR therapy, the client will be asked to focus on a specific event. Attention will be given to a negative image, belief, emotion, and body feeling related to this event and then to a positive belief indicating the issue was resolved.

While the client focuses on the upsetting event, the therapist will begin sets of side-to-side eye movements, sounds, or taps. The client will be guided to notice what comes to mind after each set. They may experience shifts in insight or changes in images, feelings, or beliefs regarding the event.

The client has complete control to stop the therapist at any point if needed. The sets of eye movements, sounds, or taps are repeated until the event becomes less disturbing.

EMDR therapy may be used within a standard talking therapy, as adjunctive therapy with a separate therapist, or as a treatment.

## How Long Does EMDR Therapy Take?

A typical EMDR therapy session lasts from 60-90 minutes. It could take one or several sessions to process one traumatic experience.

The goal of EMDR therapy is to completely process the traumatic experiences that are causing problems and to include new ones needed for full health. The amount of time it will take to complete EMDR treatment for traumatic experiences will depend upon the client's history. Complete treatment of a single EMDR trauma target involves a three-pronged protocol to alleviate the symptoms and address the complete clinical picture. The three prongs include:

- past memories
- present disturbance
- future actions

Although EMDR therapy may produce results more rapidly than other forms of therapy, speed is not the goal of therapy, and it is essential to remember that every client has different needs. For instance, one client may take weeks to establish sufficient feelings of trust (Phase 2), while another may proceed quickly through the first six phases of treatment only to reveal something even more important that needs treatment.

## "Processing" in EMDR Therapy

"Processing" does not mean talking about a traumatic experience. "Processing" means setting up a learning state that will allow experiences causing problems to be "digested" and stored appropriately in your brain. That means that what is useful to you from an experience will be learned and stored with appropriate emotions in your brain and can guide you positively in the future.

The inappropriate emotions, beliefs, and body sensations will be discarded. Negative emotions, feelings, and behaviors are generally caused by unresolved earlier experiences pushing you in the wrong direction. The goal of EMDR therapy is to leave you with the emotions, understanding, and perspectives that will lead to healthy and useful behaviors and interactions.

## Eight Phases of EMDR Therapy Treatment

There are eight phases to EMDR therapy: initial history discovery and treatment planning, preparation, assessment, desensitization, installation, body scan, closure, and reevaluation.

| | |
|---|---|
| Download Eight Phases of EMDR Therapy Infographic (English) | |
| Download Eight Phases of EMDR Therapy Infographic (Spanish) | |
| Download Eight Phases of EMDR Therapy Infographic (Urdu) | |

## Phase 1: History and Treatment Planning

This phase generally takes 1-2 sessions at the beginning of therapy and can continue throughout the therapy, especially if new problems are revealed. In the first phase of EMDR treatment, the therapist takes a thorough history of the client and develops a treatment plan. This phase will include a discussion of the specific problem that has brought him or her into therapy and the behaviors and symptoms stemming from that problem. With this information, the therapist will develop a treatment plan that defines the specific targets on which to use EMDR:

- the event(s) from the past that created the problem
- the present situations that cause distress
- the key skills or behaviors the client needs to learn for his future well-being

One of the unusual features of EMDR is that the person seeking treatment does not have to discuss any of his or her disturbing memories in detail. So, while some individuals are comfortable and even prefer giving specifics, others may present more of a general picture or outline. When the therapist asks, for example, "What event do you remember that made you feel worthless and useless?" the person may say, "It was something my brother did to me." That is all the information the therapist needs to identify and target the event with EMDR.

## Phase 2: Preparation

For most clients, this phase will take between 1-4 sessions. For others with a very traumatized background or with certain diagnoses, a longer time may be necessary. In this phase, the therapist will teach you some specific techniques so you can rapidly deal with any emotional disturbance that may arise. If you can do that, you can generally proceed to the next phase.

One of the primary goals of the preparation phase is to establish a relationship of trust between the client and the therapist. While the person does not have to go into great detail about his disturbing memories, if the EMDR client does not trust his or her therapist, he or she may not accurately report what is felt and what changes he or she is (or isn't) experiencing during the eye movements. If the client just wants to please the therapist and says they feel better when they don't, no therapy in the world will resolve that client's trauma.

During the Preparation Phase, the therapist will explain the theory of EMDR, how it is done, and what the person can expect during and after treatment. Finally, the therapist will teach the client various relaxation techniques for calming him or herself in the face of any emotional disturbance that may arise during or after a session.

In any form of therapy, it is best to look at the therapist as a facilitator or guide who needs to hear of any hurt, need, or disappointments to help achieve the common goal. EMDR therapy is a great deal more than just eye movements, and the therapist needs to know when to employ any of the needed procedures to keep the processing going. Learning these tools is an important aid for anyone. The happiest people on the planet have ways of relaxing themselves and decompressing from life's inevitable and often unsuspected stress. One goal of EMDR therapy is to ensure the client can take care of himself or herself.

## Phase 3: Assessment

In this phase, the client will be prompted to access each target in a controlled and standardized way to be effectively processed. Processing does not mean talking about it. (See the Reprocessing sections below.) The EMDR therapist identifies different parts of the target to be processed.

The first step is for the client to select a specific image or mental picture from the target event (identified during Phase One) that best represents the memory. Then he or she chooses a statement that expresses a negative self-belief associated with the event. Even if the client intellectually knows that the statement is false, he or she must focus on it. These negative beliefs are verbalizations of the disturbing emotions that still exist. Common negative cognitions include statements such as "I am helpless," "I am worthless," "I am unlovable," "I am dirty," "I am bad," etc.

The client then picks a positive self-statement that he would rather believe. This statement should incorporate an internal sense of control, such as "I am worthwhile/lovable/a good person/in control" or "I can succeed." Sometimes, when the primary emotion is fear, such as in the aftermath of a natural disaster, the negative cognition can be, "I am in danger," and the positive cognition can be, "I am safe now." "I am in danger" can be considered a negative cognition because the fear is inappropriate -- it is locked in the nervous system, but the danger is past. Positive cognition should reflect what is appropriate in the present.

The therapist will then ask the person to estimate how true a positive belief feels using the 1-to-7 Validity of Cognition (VOC) scale. "1" equals "completely false," and " 7" equals "completely true." It is essential to give a score that reflects how the person "feels," not " thinks." We may logically "know" something is wrong, but we are most driven by how it " feels."

Also, during the Assessment Phase, the person identifies the negative emotions (fear, anger) and physical sensations (tightness in the stomach, cold hands) he or she associates with the target. The client also rates the negative belief but uses a different scale called the Subjective Units of Disturbance (SUD) scale. This scale rates the feeling from 0 (no disturbance) to 10 (worst) and assesses the client's feelings.

The goal of EMDR treatment, in the following phases, is for SUD scores of disturbances to decrease while the VOC scores of positive belief increase.

Reprocessing. For a single trauma, reprocessing is generally accomplished within three sessions. If it takes longer, you should see some improvement within that time. Phases One through Three lay the groundwork for the comprehensive treatment and reprocessing of the specific targeted events. Although eye movements (or taps or tones) are used during the following three phases, they are only one component of a complex therapy. The step-by-step eight-phase approach allows the experienced, trained EMDR therapist to maximize the treatment effects for the client in a logical and standardized fashion. It also allows the client and the therapist to monitor the progress during every treatment session.

## Phase 4: Desensitization

This phase focuses on the client's disturbing emotions and sensations as measured by the SUDs rating. This phase deals with the person's responses (including other memories, insights, and associations that may arise) as the targeted event changes and its disturbing elements are resolved. This phase gives the opportunity to identify and resolve similar events that may have occurred and are associated with the target. That way, a client can surpass his or her initial goals and heal beyond expectations.

During desensitization, the therapist leads the person in sets of eye movements, sounds, or taps with appropriate shifts and changes of focus until his or her SUD-scale levels are reduced to zero (or 1 or 2 if this is more appropriate). Starting with the main target, the different associations to the memory are followed. For instance, a person may start with a horrific event and soon have other associations to it. The therapist will guide the client to a complete resolution of the target.

## Phase 5: Installation

The goal is to concentrate on and increase the strength of the positive belief that the client has identified to replace his or her original negative belief. For example, the client might begin with a mental image of being beaten up by his or her father and a negative belief of "I am powerless." During the Desensitization

Phase, that client will have reprocessed the terror of that childhood event and fully realized that as an adult, he or she now has strength and choices that were not there when he or she was young.

During this fifth phase of treatment, that person's positive cognition, "I am now in control," will be strengthened and installed. How deeply the person believes that positive cognition is then measured using the Validity of Cognition (VOC) scale. The goal is for the person to accept the full truth of his or her positive self-statement at a level of 7 (completely true).

Fortunately, just as EMDR cannot make anyone shed appropriate negative feelings, it cannot make the person believe anything positive that is not appropriate either. So, if the person is aware that he or she needs to learn some new skill, such as self-defense training, to be truly in control of the situation, the validity of that positive belief will rise only to the corresponding level, such as a 5 or 6 on the VOC scale.

# Phase 6: Body Scan

After the positive cognition has been strengthened and installed, the therapist will ask the person to bring the original target event to mind and see if any residual tension is noticed in the body. If so, these physical sensations are then targeted for reprocessing.

Evaluations of thousands of EMDR sessions indicate that there is a physical response to unresolved thoughts. This finding has been supported by independent studies of memory indicating that when a person is negatively affected by trauma, information about the traumatic event is stored in body memory (motoric memory), rather than narrative memory and retains the negative emotions and physical sensations of the original event. However, when that information is processed, it can then move to narrative (or verbalizable) memory, and the body sensations and negative feelings associated with it disappear.

Therefore, an EMDR session is not considered successful until the client can bring up the original target without feeling any body tension. Positive self-beliefs are important, but they have to be believed on more than just an intellectual level.

## Phase 7: Closure

Ends every treatment session. Closure ensures that the person leaves feeling better at the end of each session than at the beginning.

If the processing of the traumatic target event is not complete in a single session, the therapist will assist the client in using a variety of self-calming techniques in order to regain a sense of equilibrium. Throughout the EMDR session, the client has been in control (for instance, the client is instructed that it is okay to raise a hand in the "stop" gesture at any time) and it is essential that the client continue to feel in control outside the therapist's office.

He or she is also briefed on what to expect between sessions (some processing may continue, some new material may arise), how to use a journal to record these experiences, and what calming techniques could be used to self-soothe in the client's life outside of the therapy session.

## Phase 8: Reevaluation

Opens every new session. The Reevaluation Phase guides the therapist through the treatment plans needed to deal with the client's problems. As with any form of sound therapy, the Reevaluation Phase is vital to determine the success of the treatment over time. Although clients may feel relief almost immediately with EMDR, it is as essential to complete the eight phases of treatment as it is to complete an entire course of treatment with antibiotics.

## The Role of Past, Present, and Future Templates

EMDR therapy is not complete until attention has been brought to the past memories contributing to the problem, the disturbing present situations, and what skills the client may need for the future.

# Resources

Excerpts above from: F. Shapiro & M.S. Forrest (2004) EMDR: The Breakthrough Therapy for Anxiety, Stress and Trauma. New York: Basic Books.

http://www.perseusbooksgroup.com/perseus-cgi-bin/display/0-465-04301$-1

# Special Thanks
## TO THOSE WHO HELPED SHAPE ME

## Joan

Dear Joan, my beloved elder sister,

I express my heartfelt gratitude to you for being one of the rare individuals who showered their younger siblings with genuine love and affection. As we continue to mature, we now comprehend the sacrifices you made and the desires you selflessly put aside. Our souls are forever grateful for the profound impact you had on our lives, even in the smallest of ways. Thank you for being our savior and guiding light.

# *Tiny*

It's somewhat amusing as I reflect upon our past, but now I find myself compelled to express my gratitude for all the tough love you bestowed upon me. From the countless beatings to the moments when you pushed me against the wall and made me fight, and even when I knocked you out (Jerry Cooney), I realize now the profound favor you did for me. You made me resilient; you turned me into a fearless individual, and because of this unconventional brotherly love, I have become the strong, accomplished woman I am today. I refuse to tolerate any nonsense, and for that, I thank you from the bottom of my heart.

## Toni Dovi

I wanted to take a moment to express my deepest gratitude to you, even though I never had the opportunity to thank you in person. In my time at Fox Lane. Middle School in Bedford Hills, you were my guidance counselor, and it was through your guidance that my life took a remarkable turn. You provided me with a path out of the depths of despair and sent me to a place to grow, live, and experience love. It is because of your unwavering support that I am still here today.

The seeds of hope and encouragement that you planted in my heart took time to flourish, but when they finally did, they grew into the most beautiful orchids, or rather, lotuses. I will forever hold in my memory everything you did for me. The countless hours you spent just listening to me and the genuine care and compassion you showed me have had a profound impact on my life. It is because of your belief in me, your recognition of my worth, and the chance you gave me that I am standing where I am today.

I am eternally grateful for your guidance, your saving grace, and your unwavering belief in my potential. Thank you for being the light that guided me out of darkness and for seeing the worth in me when I couldn't see it in myself. Your impact on my life is immeasurable, and I will carry your kindness and support with me always.

# *Nanette*

She is a remarkable woman, selfless and dedicated to helping others feel worthy and wanted. Through her belief in others and her guidance, I have become who I am today. The seed she planted in Fox Lane Middle School many years ago has finally grown, and I am grateful for her teachings on how to be a teacher/Entrepreneur.

Nanette is truly a blessing, not just to me but too many others whose lives she has touched. She embodies the qualities of an extraordinary being, someone who brings light and inspiration to those around her.

Thank you, Nanette, for being there when I needed and for planting the seeds that have helped me become the women I am today. Your impact is immeasurable, and your dedication to your students is commendable.

# Dr. William Sobel

I wanted to take a moment to express my deepest gratitude to you for the impactful role you played in my life. It's amazing how, for some inexplicable reason, certain people enter and exit our lives at just the right moments. You came into my life when I was at my lowest, when I couldn't see a way forward and couldn't hear the support of others. But you saw me when I was blind, and you heard me when I was deaf to the world around me.

During a time when I felt like nobody cared, you showed me that I was not alone. Your presence, your patience, and your quiet understanding made an immense difference in my life. You provided me with the caring and support that I desperately needed at that time. Your kindness and compassion were a lifeline for me, and I will forever be grateful for that.

So, thank you, Doc, for being there for me and for being there for so many others. You are a true lifesaver, not just in the metaphorical sense, but in the way you have touched and saved the lives of those you have encountered. Your kindness, compassion, and support are invaluable, and I am forever grateful for your presence in my life.

# Dr. Rob

Thank you for showing me that life's struggles can make me

stronger too.

You held my hand when I stumbled, never letting me fall.

Your unwavering support, my heart will forever recall.

In the depths of despair, you were my beacon of hope.

A friend like no other, with you, I could always cope.

You saw my flaws and imperfections, yet you still believed,

That love could heal the wounds and help my soul be relieved.

Your honesty, a rare gem, cutting through deceit and lies,

You opened my eyes to the truth, unveiling life's disguise.

Through the storms we weathered, our bond only grew

stronger, A bond so genuine, it could withstand anything, last

longer.

In the darkest hours, you showed me the power of a smile,

How it could ease the burdens, even for just a little while.

Your love was like a soothing balm, mending my broken soul,

Together, we faced the challenges, making me whole.

So, thank you, dear Rob, for being my guiding light,

For teaching me to face my fears and never give up the fight.

Forever grateful for your love and wisdom, I'll always be,

For you've shown me the beauty in embracing authenticity.

# Noelle Damon,
## LCSWR, DAAETS

In the depths of darkness and sorrow's grip,

A path littered with trials, my fate did trip.

But oh, the gratitude that now cascades,

For you, my guide, who unveiled clarity's shades.


With each step taken, my flame rekindled,

Exhaling despair, my spirit re-enriddled.

A smile now adorns my weary face,

All thanks to you, who restored my grace.

You, a beacon of light that guides my way,

Infusing my journey with brilliance each day.

No longer lost, I sail with renewed might,

For you illuminate my voyage with radiant light.

# *Mother and Father Cole*

In my journey of pain and perseverance, I have come to realize the profound importance of forgiveness for one's own healing. So, dear Mom and Dad, I extend my forgiveness to you for the things you were unable to give me in this lifetime. In a strange way, I even express gratitude for the hardships and heartaches, as they have shaped me into the person I am today - someone who can empathize and support others who find themselves trapped in their own struggles, feeling hopeless. I only hope that you have found happiness in your current circumstances and have learned the invaluable lesson of self-forgiveness, or rather, how to become better individuals. Thank you for what you could not do for me or provide me with, for it is precisely because of those absences that I have grown stronger.

# *Mom and Dad Messina*

I express my heartfelt gratitude to Mom and Dad Messina for embodying the divine role of my biological parents. Your unwavering love and constant presence in my life have been a profound blessing. Thank you for being my unwavering pillars of support, for nurturing my dreams, and for accepting me wholeheartedly.

# *Ray*

My dearest love, your words touch my soul,

Gratitude fills my heart, making it whole.

Through thick and thin, we've stood side by side,

Facing life's challenges, with love as our guide.

You've been my rock, my shelter in the storm,

Nurturing me when I was weak, keeping me warm.

In sickness and in health, we've weathered the test,

Emerging stronger, our bond truly blessed.

Together, we've faced heartaches and strife,

Yet our love remains steadfast, igniting new life.

Accepting each other, flaws and all,

Our love grows deeper, standing tall.

I cherish every moment spent with you,

And I can't imagine a life with someone new.

So hand in hand, let's embark on this quest,

Building a future, a sandbox we'll nest.

With you by my side, I have no fear,

For our love will conquer, crystal clear.

Together, as one, we'll create something grand,

A testament to the strength of our love, hand in hand.

## My dear friends

Thank you to the friends that have been by my side through thick and thin. For calling me on my shit and for telling me what I needed to hear not what I wanted to hear. Your honesty and support have been a guiding light in my life, helping me navigate through challenges and celebrate successes. I am grateful for your unwavering friendship and for always being there, no matter the circumstances. Together, we have shared laughter, tears, and unforgettable memories that have shaped who we are today. Here's to many more years of friendship and cherished moments ahead.

## Elite Publications

I would like to express my gratitude for the invaluable assistance in enabling numerous individuals to share their stories and amplifying their reach. Your contribution to my project is deeply appreciated, and I eagerly anticipate the promising future that lies ahead with your continued involvement.

# *Thank you to my and our abusers*

Thank you for casting your darkness and self-centeredness upon me. Thank you for the pain and suffering that you instilled within me. For today, I stand in front of you, stronger, braver, and more committed than ever to making the wrongs in this world right. This is an injustice, and I dare you to stop me.

Your actions may have tried to break me, but they only fueled the fire within me. I have transformed my pain into power, and I will use that power to fight against the injustices that plague our society. Your attempt to silence me has only given me a louder voice, a voice that will not be silenced until justice is served.

I will not allow your darkness to define me. Instead, I will use it as a catalyst for change. I will be a beacon of light, shining on the darkest corners of society, exposing the injustices that are often hidden and ignored.

You may have thought that by hurting me/us, you could control me/us. But you were wrong. You have only made me stronger, more determined, and more resilient. I will no longer be a victim.

I will rise above the pain and become a survivor, a warrior for justice.

I am no longer defined by the pain you inflicted upon me. I am defined by my resilience, my courage, and my unwavering commitment to make a difference. I will continue to stand up, speak out, and fight for justice, not just for myself, but for all those who have suffered at the hands of abusers.

No longer will I allow your actions to control my life. I am taking back my power, and I will use it to create a world where no one else has to endure what I went through. I will be the change I wish to see in the world, and I will not be stopped.

So, thank you, abusers, for inadvertently pushing me to become the person I am today. A person who will not be silenced, who will not be broken, and who will not stop until justice is served.

# "Our Chosen Sun"

Ray, Brett and Maggie today.

# The beginning...

## "Every day is a NEW DAY!"
Maggie wins Gold for the USA, Cardiff Wales

# *About the Author*

## MAGGIE COLE MESSINA

Maggie Cole Messina is a resilient individual who has faced adversity from a young age. Born in Nyack, NY, she grew up in poverty and spent most of her childhood in the NYS Foster care system. Despite her challenges, Maggie was determined not to become another statistic and fought to overcome the obstacles in her path.

Maggie's love for sports was met with resistance due to her gender. Whether it was basketball, softball, or football, she faced exclusion and discrimination. Despite these setbacks,

Maggie remained determined to find her purpose and make a difference.

After graduating high school, Maggie found herself homeless for many months due to flaws in the foster care system. She longed for safety and security, but her life lacked direction. However, she felt a burning desire for a meaningful purpose, which led her to martial arts and advocacy work.

Maggie became a speaker, addressing various vital topics such as bullying and child abuse. Her personal experiences and resilience allowed her to connect with audiences and inspire change.

In 2023, Maggie's selflessness and continued support for the state of New York and the United States were recognized when she received the lifetime presidential award from President Joe Biden. She also received several congressional awards for her outstanding contributions.

Maggie is a genuine diamond in the rough, and her journey is far from over. Her determination to right the wrongs and make a positive impact serves as an inspiration to others.

She is just getting started on her mission to create a better world.

For more information about Maggie and her other published works, please visit https://www.makingmaggie.com/.

Made in United States
North Haven, CT
06 May 2024

52190047R00104